THE ENCHANTED WREATH

A FANTASY FAIRY TALE RETELLING OF THE
ENCHANTED WREATH

THE NEVERTOLD FAIRY TALE NOVELLAS
BOOK THREE

BRITTANY FICHTER

To Chimaine,

You are the sunshine that binds the people around you together. With every day I know you, you grow more beautiful, and it's an honor and a privilege to call you my friend and sister-in-Christ.

POST TENEBRAS LUX

After darkness...

...light.

TO THE HONORABLE KING EVERARD AND QUEEN ISABELLE,

To the Honorable King Everard and Queen Isabelle,

Though it isn't included in the tale itself, Peter says that the events which inspired the story we're telling today nearly started a war. The witch described in the story not only committed terrible atrocities from within the kingdom, but from without as well, leading numerous rulers to believe that the evils committed against them were committed by one another. It was the body of benevolent fae (the ones we mentioned in the last story) that intervened and ultimately spared many from bloodshed.

This is probably my favorite of the stories we've told so far. Probably because the prince reminds me of a certain carefree soul I fell in love with not so long ago...

But I digress.

Yours respectfully,
Wendy Darling Pan

Once upon a time in a faraway land...

ONE

Gisele hefted the picnic basket from one hip to the other as she walked, trying to find a more comfortable position to carry it. It didn't matter which side she held it on, however. The basket was simply too large and too full to be anything other than awkward.

"Did we really need to bring this much food?" she puffed as they began up yet another hill. "We'll be home by supper."

"It's not a short walk to the village from the house," Gisele's stepmother said evenly. She had a thin parasol on her left arm and her right draped over Gisele's father's arm. "I wanted to make sure we had more than enough to eat."

Gisele bit back a retort about how her stepmother could carry the food herself if she wanted it so much. But it would have been disrespectful, and Gisele's mother had raised her better than that.

"I'm still surprised you wanted to come to the parade at all," Simone said as the family joined the wider road where the hundreds of other country dwellers also trekked toward the village.

"And why is that?" Gisele asked with a groan as she transferred the basket to her other hip again.

"You seem to enjoy keeping the house so much." Gisele's stepsister gave her a knowing smile. "I didn't think something like this would bring you pleasure."

"He's my prince, too," Gisele said, trying not to sound out of breath. This basket was really heavy. "It's not every day royalty comes to Shadeling."

"She's right," Gisele's father said. He paused to adjust the bundle of wood he carried on his back, which he hoped to sell to one of the wealthier village families while they were there. "I believe the last time one of the royal family members passed through was about four years ago when the king was overseeing the faeries' treatment for the corn blight." He looked down at his wife. "Are you able to finish this hill, Adrienne?"

"Yes, but I need to catch my breath." She sent Gisele a saccharine smile. "I don't know how you two became so hardy. Simone and I have lived in this area all our lives, and we've never been strengthened by the air as you two are."

Gisele once again repressed a sharp reply, this one about how actual work would do that to a person. As if hearing her thoughts, her father gave her a slight frown and shook his head.

Unfortunately, as was often the case, it seemed Gisele's eyes had betrayed her. Her mother had once said Gisele's eyes were more open than a book, in that one didn't need to know one's letters to read her. To her father, she might as well have spoken the rebuttal aloud.

The family came to rest on the side of the road, where her father helped her stepmother sink onto the ground, and Gisele gratefully let the picnic basket fall before collapsing beside it. It wasn't quite as comfortable as she'd hoped, however. The spring grass, which was usually soft and green this time of year, had already been flattened by the hundreds of feet that had trod on it earlier that day.

"When is the prince supposed to arrive?" Simone asked, twirling her own parasol as she watched their neighbors walk past them. Gisele knew most of them by name and would have called out to them, except she had little desire to have any deep conversations where the newer members of her family could hear. So she restrained herself to a mere wave whenever they were greeted by the passers-by. She would have far more freedom once they reached the village.

"About midday," Gisele's father said. "Which means we need to keep moving if we wish to get a good place. Are you ready, darling?"

"I'm already rested," Adrienne said, allowing Gisele's father to pull her to her feet. "You're right, though. We should go before we're left at the back of the crowd."

That wouldn't happen, and Gisele knew it, which was one of the reasons she had chosen to attend the parade with her family rather than her friends. For as mad as it sounded to explain it, Simone and Adrienne seemed to have a magic of their own, the kind that would elicit bows and favors from even happily married men—men who would often look confused and a little disoriented when the interaction was done. And though Gisele was hesitant to believe such nonsense, she'd seen it too many times to think otherwise.

The mother and daughter were beautiful. Not even Gisele, who had seen all she wanted and more of their ugly hearts, could deny that. And both of them, Simone in particular, seemed to have increased in beauty even over the last few months. It was fairly disgusting and made them less than popular with the village women. Although their lack of popularity probably had something to do with their strange pull on the men—and their obvious enjoyment of it—as well. Both women had striking red hair of the silkiest texture Gisele had ever seen. Their eyes were bright green, and their skin rosy and flawless. Their forms were delicate and soft, perfectly rounded in all the right places.

Everything Gisele was not.

Gisele had never thought herself homely by any means. As a child, she'd been told she was quite pretty. But her light brown hair didn't stand a chance of being noticed beside that of her stepsister's vivid red, and her figure, while slim, was solid and strong from years of helping her father cut and carry wood in the forest. She couldn't afford dainty shoulders or soft hands, and her skin was plastered with freckles and as tan—in Simone's words—as pale leather.

In essence, she was as water placed beside cherry wine when she stood beside the incomparable Simone.

This comparison didn't bother Gisele in general. While she wouldn't have minded being the town's favorite, such wouldn't put food on the table or purchase nails with which to fix their chicken coop. And in general, she stayed as far away from her family in public as possible. But on days like this, when the family was forced to come to the village together, Gisele felt the gap between herself and her step-sister seem to widen, and all too often, she was beginning to feel as though she was becoming invisible.

Today, wearing her best dress, which was one Simone no longer wanted, she felt that gap more sharply than ever.

They finally reached the outskirts of the village about fifteen minutes later. The crowds had already filled the small streets until they seemed like they might burst. As usual, however, Adrienne and Simone were able to part the crowd as though they were slicing it with a knife. The two women smiled and simpered as they led Gisele and her father to the front, and Gisele wondered–not for the first time–how men were so oblivious so as not to see through them.

More importantly, how her father hadn't seen through them.

Once the two women had claimed a place along the edge of the main street, Gisele moaned slightly as she put the picnic basket down. Her arms and back, though strong from years of woodcutting, were somehow still sore from the near hour-long walk with her burden.

"Gisele," Adrienne called over her shoulder, "fetch me a waterskin. And then be a darling and move the basket where I can sit on it."

Gisele glanced at her father, but as usual these days, he was staring off into the distance, appearing completely unaware of everything around him.

"And when you're done," Simone added, "I'd like you to buy me one of those little sweet pies from that shop over there." She pointed to the other side of the road. "They have my favorite."

"That's across the road and through another crowd," Gisele said as she handed her stepmother the waterskin. "I'm not going to get you a pastry when I just carried six in this basket over several miles."

For a brief moment, Simone's angelic smile was replaced by a narrowed gaze.

Unwilling to be unnerved, Gisele stared right back.

Finally, Simone's glare changed to a smirk. "I'm not sure why you're putting up such a fuss," she said with a shrug. "You said you didn't want to see the prince after all." She looked at her mother. "Didn't she say that, Mother?"

"Yes, you did." Adrienne pulled two coins from her coin purse and handed them to Gisele. "Go get Simone the pie, then buy one for yourself."

Gisele looked at her father, who was still staring absently at a building across the road, when a blessed voice called her name from behind.

"April!" Gisele whirled around and called back to her friend. "Stay there! I'll come to you!" She turned and began to pick her way through the crowd until she reached April two buildings over, pretending she couldn't hear the cries of protest she left behind.

"Thank you!" she said as she joined her friend's family at their slightly less-advantageous spot near the street. "I was about to sink myself into trouble."

"They're being awful again, aren't they?" April made a face in the direction of Gisele's relatives.

"They're being exhausting," Gisele said, stretching her shoulders and neck. "Apparently, today, I'm a workhorse."

"Have you talked to your father about it, dear?" April's mother asked, her face pinched with concern. She had been one of Gisele's mother's closest friends when her mother had still lived, and she often treated Gisele as though she were another daughter in addition to their five. She and her husband had even offered to let Gisele live with them after Gisele's father had married Adrienne.

Unfortunately, with five daughters and no sons, they had little to spare, and as much as Gisele should have loved living with them above all else, she couldn't bring herself to tax their resources further.

"He's been made aware," Gisele gave her a grim smile. "Now, tell me. What do you know of the prince?"

Fran, April's younger sister, smirked. "Unlike that Lord...what was his name? The one who came through a few months ago? Oh, yes. Lord Massy. Unlike him, Prince Julien is supposed to actually be handsome."

"Lord Massy wasn't that ugly," one of April's older sisters, Tori, said gently. "He was just..."

"Ugly." April looked at Gisele and shook her head. "He was ugly."

"It would have helped if he'd smiled," Tori amended. "I've never seen a man look so sour for so long."

"What happened to your arm?" April asked, taking Gisele's arm and holding it up to examine it. "It looks like you burned it."

"I did."

"But how?"

"With tea."

"With...what?" April frowned.

Gisele rolled her eyes and glanced down at April's mother to make sure she wasn't listening. The story would only upset her.

She pulled April aside and lowered her voice. "I was ironing a gown for Adrienne–"

"She can't iron her own gowns?" April asked hotly.

"She had a headache, apparently," Gisele said. "Anyhow, I was ironing, and it seems I was too close to Simone's cup of tea. She reached over me to pick it up and splashed a good deal of it on my arm."

"You should have gotten her right back with the iron," April grumbled.

"I'm eighteen years old," Gisele said wryly. "I wasn't about to get into a shoving match with my stepsister."

April opened her mouth to no doubt make a sharp reply, but the crowd let out a roar at the far end of the street.

"He must be coming!" Fran cried. She stretched up on the tips of her toes. "I can't see him! Can you see him?"

Gisele and April grinned at one another. Fran, who was fourteen, had dreams of grandeur that could outshine any girl her age.

Gisele entertained fewer daydreams than her friend's sister, but she did try to peek over the heads of the crowd as well. Unfortunately, she found that while she was of average height, she couldn't see any better than Fran could. From the way the roar began to make its way closer to where they were standing, however, she knew the prince must be coming near. Hopefully, she would catch a glimpse of him.

Why Gisele wanted to glimpse the prince so badly, she didn't exactly know. Unlike Fran, she didn't entertain delusions of his falling desperately in love with her at first sight and whisking her away to his castle. But to see him would be a treat, a spark in her otherwise uneventful life that had become even more uneventful since her father had remarried.

And, a small voice inside whispered, if she was honest, she would–just for a moment–like to be seen by him, too.

"Gisele?"

Gisele looked down to find a small girl at her side. She immediately recognized the pale messy hair, thin face, and big blue eyes. Blue eyes that looked scared. Gisele knelt and took the little girl's hands.

"Michelle, what's wrong?"

"It's my mummy," the little girl said, blinking back tears. "She's hurt, and she needs someone big, quick."

Gisele stood and cast another hopeful glance in the direction the prince would be riding from. But she was still unable to see him.

"I asked Auntie Adrienne already, but she said to find you," the little girl continued.

Gisele sighed and used her handkerchief to wipe the little girl's tears away. "Let's go see your mummy."

"Where are you going?" April called out over the din.

"I've got to go help Becca!" Gisele called back.

"But she's *Adrienne's* cousin!"

Gisele simply shrugged and let the little girl lead the way as the roar of the crowd nearly deafened them all.

GISELE TRIED NOT to feel bitter as she followed the little girl down several alleyways to the streets of cottages that were small and run-down. April had been right. Becca *was* Adrienne's cousin. She and her husband had been wealthy landowners until recently, when he was killed in a hunting accident, and the will revealed that his gambling debts were far more than their gold could pay. The land had been sold, and Becca had moved herself and her small daughter into the only house they could afford. To make matters more complicated, Becca had discovered soon after that she was with child.

And Adrienne wanted nothing to do with them. She had, however, been able to assuage any possible familial guilt she might have been cursed with by suggesting that Gisele help them.

"They're your family, too, now," she'd told Gisele several months before. "And you're so resourceful. Surely you can find it in your heart to help."

As Gisele made her way through the broken gate into the cottage, which was little more than a shack, she felt her heart sink. It was worse than it had been the last time she'd visited. Filth and grime covered every inch of the floors and the walls. To her relief, the windows, which had not the luxury of real glass, were still covered by the fat-smeared parchment Gisele had tacked up last time to try and keep out the wind. The bed was nothing more than a straw mattress covered in a pile of grimy blankets, and piled on the table were several dirty bowls and mugs. Becca herself lay on her back on the floor.

"Becca, what happened?" Gisele asked as she hurried to help the woman sit up. It was difficult and rather awkward, as Becca's middle section was now quite rotund, but together, they managed to ease her into the rocking chair by the fire.

"I was...trying to catch the animal fat...the way Mrs. Phelps taught me to do...to save for later," Becca gasped between breaths. "But I spilled some...and slipped." She let out a cry as Gisele's hands felt up and down her spine. "Oh, that hurts!"

Gisele leaned back on her heels and frowned.

"As much as I hate to say it, I think we need to call the physician."

Becca's eyes, the same color as her daughter's, flew open wide. "Oh, no! I'm still paying him for the last time Michelle got sick! I can't–"

"I can." Gisele pulled two coins out of her little purse and folded Becca's fingers over them.

"No." Becca shook her head, her jaw trembling. "I couldn't ask you–"

"Before you get upset, don't for a moment think that I'm going to leave you here alone and in pain. Besides," Gisele couldn't help letting a grin slip, "it's Adrienne's money. I was supposed to use it to buy Simone a pie." She put the coins in Becca's hand. "But from what Adrienne has told me, we *must* find it in our hearts to help."

Becca stared at the coins in her hand and sighed. Then

she looked up at Gisele. "I don't understand. Why did you allow your father to marry my cousin?"

Gisele snorted. "Oh, there was no *allowance*. I begged him not to."

Becca frowned. "I assume by that point, he'd been captivated by a pair of brilliant green eyes."

Gisele pulled her little silver comb from her purse and set to brushing the knots out of Michelle's hair. "You see my situation."

Becca shook her head. "I'm not blind to what a burden I am to the family. And I won't pretend I have the skills my daughter needs for us to survive in this world." She looked back up at Gisele. "But I wouldn't trade places with you for the world. There's..." Her frown deepened, and she leaned forward, her voice dropping to a whisper. "Something isn't right with Adrienne and Simone. I don't know what. I can't say. But you...you watch yourself around them. Yes? And promise me something, Gisele." She took Gisele's hand in her own and squeezed so tightly that it hurt.

"Do whatever you can to get out of that house. You hear?" Her pale eyes suddenly burned with a passion Gisele had never seen in the woman. "You're not going to be in that house forever. And though the two of them will try to keep you there, I have faith that–"

"Becca," Gisele interrupted, "it's really nothing to upset yourself–"

"Gisele. Listen to me. If anyone can escape," Becca repeated, enunciating every word, her eyes still ablaze, "It's. You."

AFTER CALLING the physician and then cleaning and tidying as much as she could, Gisele set out to take advantage of the remaining daylight to find her way back to her family. But when she reached the town square, they were nowhere to be seen. Nor were they to be found when she returned to the place they'd stood on the street.

They had left without her.

Still aching from her earlier trek with the picnic basket, Gisele took comfort in the knowledge that if they had already gone, at least she wouldn't have to lug the ridiculous basket back home. As the sun set, however, and darkness filled the world with various shades of deepening blues, Gisele recalled Becca's insistent cries that Adrienne and Simone would try to keep her under their thumb.

Gisele didn't doubt that for a moment. Why would they give up the free labor Gisele had obviously come to be?

Stranger yet, however, was Becca's insistence that Gisele would indeed succeed in escaping the place that had once been her home.

As she came to the top of a ridge, Gisele came to a stop, staring down at the wide countryside spread out before her. She could leave right now. She could take another path and go anywhere she wished. Should she desire to go to the end of the world, neither Adrienne nor Simone would be there to stop her.

But how would she survive? She had little money and no

provisions, no living relatives she knew of, and no knowledge of the world beyond her village's borders. And as much as she might wish it otherwise, the world was not a friendly place to a lone young woman of common birth.

No, she would do best to go back to her father's cottage and continue to ponder her plight there.

As she walked, however, she found that her own optimism did not match Becca's. The last year had been a dark one. In it, Gisele had lost her mother and had essentially become a servant in her own home. Despite all of this, Becca seemed sure Gisele would escape the tyranny of her stepmother and stepsister soon enough.

Gisele, however, wasn't so sure.

TWO

Gisele stood and wiped the sweat from her brow with her handkerchief. A cool breeze fluttered by, and she closed her eyes to soak it up as her father's axe continued to ring through the hills. Then it stopped, and Gisele opened her eyes.

"It's a warm one for early spring," her father said, mopping his own brow with his sleeve.

"Mmm," Gisele responded. Usually, she would have added something to the effect of how it might be a good growing season for the garden or how they might be able to cut an extra store of firewood if it dried faster. But after the previous day's events, Gisele found herself short-tempered and wondering if her father would even notice.

After a moment of silence, he lifted his axe and began splitting logs again. Gisele had gathered the wood he'd already cut and was loading it onto their cart when her father surprised her by putting down his axe again.

"I wanted to, um, thank you for yesterday. For helping

out with Becca, I mean. Adrienne appreciated it. It meant a lot to her. I would have helped, had I known, but I didn't get to see the prince, either. She needed me to, um, see to some purchases."

"Ah, yes. She appreciated it so much that she took two of my coins as payment for giving hers to her sick cousin who needed a physician." Gisele kept her eyes firmly on her work. "She appreciated it *ever* so much."

"Becca needed a physician?"

"Yes. Because she'd fallen on the ground and couldn't get up." Gisele finally turned to face her father. "You *do* know she's with child, don't you?"

"Oh." Gisele's father swallowed and looked at the ground. "Well, as I said, Adrienne—"

Gisele threw a piece of wood into the cart with a little more force than was necessary. "Father, you can try as much as you like to make excuses for her. But there is simply no justification for Adrienne ignoring her pregnant cousin's cry for help."

"Well, you were there," her father said, picking up his axe again. "And with the prince coming—"

"Simone has a suitor."

"But a prince would help the family more." Her father turned to her with pleading eyes. Eyes that pleaded for her to understand...that had been pleading since he'd begun courting the woman. But Gisele was done understanding.

"And what about me?"

Her father split another log. "What about you?"

"What if *I* wanted to see the prince? Or better yet, what if I wanted to marry him?"

Her father stopped working again and looked at her as though she'd suggested she wanted to eat frogs.

"I know," Gisele said, her voice suddenly trembling, "that I'm not as pretty as Simone. The same way I know Mother wasn't as pretty as Adrienne."

Her father threw the axe into the stump so it stuck. "Now, you stop right there!" He pointed an accusing finger at her, but Gisele stormed on.

"I'm not blind. I can see that my stepsister and even my stepmother outshine me in every aspect."

"I...I never said that," her father stuttered.

"But what kills me is that I know that you see what they're really like. Who they really are. If you didn't, you wouldn't suddenly need to travel away from home so often as you do now."

"I go to sell the wood!" he protested.

"You go to escape! And worse, as you turn a blind eye to...to all they lack, you leave me behind to clean it up for you!" Gisele felt herself suddenly dangerously close to tears. But she ground her teeth, refusing to let them fall. "If Mother could see the way you've changed–"

"Oh, and how have I changed?"

"You left me in the village last night! I had to walk home alone through miles of wild land by myself! I didn't get home until an hour after dark!"

To his credit, her father flushed a deep scarlet. Then he tried to wave her away. "You're a strong girl," he muttered. "I knew you'd find your way just fine."

"You wouldn't so much as let Mother walk to the edge of the property after dark! You always said there were too many wild animals that come up from the woods. But now that you've replaced Mother, you abandoned me–"

"That's *enough*!" her father roared.

There was a danger in her father's voice that Gisele had rarely, if ever, heard before. Knowing she had pushed him to his limit, she simply glared at him as he glared at her, each breathing hard as the wind whistled quietly around them.

Finally, after another minute, her father shook his head once and then went back to chopping.

THEY CHOPPED IN SILENCE UNTIL, a few hours later, it began to rain.

"Hurry," her father said, "before the wood gets wet."

Gisele didn't need to be told, however. She grabbed the wool blanket out of the cart and threw it over the wood. Her father took the donkey from the tree to which they'd tied him and hooked him to the cart. Then they began the long trek back to the house, the ground beneath them growing more slippery with each step.

At first, they seemed to make good time. A few minutes later, however, her father let out a cry and grabbed onto the cart for support. Gisele ran to his side to find him clutching his ankle.

"Slipped in a blasted hole," he said through clenched teeth. "You'll have to lead her."

Gisele grabbed the reins from her father's hand and set to leading the donkey up the slick path, her father holding onto the cart for support as he walked. This took them twice the amount of time it should have to return, and by the time they reached the barn, they were both soaked through.

"Go inside," Gisele told her father. "I'll unhook her."

Her father watched her for a moment before nodding. "Thank you," he said in a husky voice. Then he limped toward the door that led from the barn straight into the cottage.

Gisele took her time drying and brushing the donkey. With the presence of their two cows, chickens, pig, cats, and the dog, the little barn was comfortably warm. It was also blessedly quiet.

"How do you think I'll have to earn my supper tonight?" Gisele asked the ginger cat who climbed onto her shoulders. "If it wouldn't make them so happy, I'd just as well come out and eat my supper with you."

Unfortunately, Gisele's stomach did eventually rumble and drive her into the house. Her clothes had mostly dried while she was in the barn, but her braid was still quite wet, and she looked forward to brushing it out and drying it after she changed clothes.

"Ah, Gisele! Just who we were looking for."

Gisele held back the sigh she deeply wanted to release at the sound of her stepmother's voice.

"Your father seems to have forgotten his axe in the excitement of his accident. Would you be so kind as to run and fetch it for him?"

"I was thinking," Gisele's father said, in a low voice, "that Gisele's just nearly dried off. Maybe...maybe you. Or Simone could get it?"

If this request insulted or enraged Adrienne, she didn't show it. "I would love to, darling," she cooed instead, "but I'm nearly done with dinner. And Simone is waiting for Lord Andersly to come courting. Gisele, you don't mind, do you? You're already wet as it is."

Gisele held her stepmother's gaze for an eternal moment. Then she looked at her father.

"It would...be a big help," her father finally said, not meeting her eyes. "Can't have the blade rusting and all."

"No, you're right," Gisele echoed, forcing a fierce smile. "We can't have that."

THREE

The walk back to where Gisele and her father had been splitting logs took far longer than it should have, largely because what had been a steady rain quickly became a downpour. And though the spring had been unseasonably warm, Gisele was shivering violently by the time she found the axe.

But when she put her hand out to yank it from the log where her father had stuck the blade, something was on it. Three somethings.

Squinting to see through the buckets of water that continued pouring from the sky, Gisele finally made out that there were three small birds perched on the axe's handle, huddled together as one.

There was a branch above the stump that sheltered the axe from the full force of the downpour, and Gisele could only guess that the little birds had believed themselves to be perched on another, sturdier branch beneath.

"Little ones, go back to your nest!" Gisele called over the

storm, waving her hand at them. But the birds didn't budge. She looked around, hoping their nest and their mother were nearby so she might move them to where they needed to be. But there was no nest in sight, and Gisele couldn't imagine they would last much longer out in the storm.

"Here," she said, holding out her skirt with one hand and shooing the birds into it with the other. She expected them to hop or fly away or ignore her the way they had done the first time. Ideally, they would return to wherever they were supposed to be. But instead of trying to escape, the little birds allowed her to scoop them into her skirt.

Gisele stared at them for a moment before remembering to retrieve the axe as well. She had the axe, which was what she had come for, but she now had three little birds as well.

A crack of thunder from above made her jump. No matter where she went, she couldn't stay here. She squinted up at the path to find that it was now invisible in the rain. So going home was no longer an option. But where else was there to go?

Anger that had been stoked the night before rekindled as she remembered the sinking feeling of realization that she had been abandoned.

She couldn't sit here and feel sorry for herself, though. She needed to *do* something other than stand in the rain. Then, as she looked around, she was struck with a memory from when she was small. Her mother had brought her along as she and Gisele's father had split wood, and during their midday meal, they had explored the vicinity, pretending to be adventurers. Gisele remembered it as though it had all happened yesterday.

She turned left and trudged through the soaked under-brush toward the large rock outcropping that *should* be nearby.

Sure enough, a few minutes later, she found it. And just as she remembered, there was a small cave within.

"Be thankful I remembered this place," she told the little birds as she set them gently on a dry rock. Her teeth chattered as she talked, but she continued to address the little birds as though they could understand her. For some reason, it made her situation seem far less lonely than it threatened to be. And if she didn't talk to someone, she just might cry.

"One wouldn't believe I changed cloaks before leaving," she continued, hugging herself as she looked around. "I'm nearly soaked through." To her relief, there was a large pile of dry leaves from the autumn before that had blown into the cave's entrance. As much as she was able, she cleared a space on the floor and used a stone to dig a small pit. Then she surrounded it with as many rocks as she could find. After scrounging about the cave, she was again grateful to find a number of dry sticks. Arranging them within the little pit, she took a sharp piece of flint and a small bit of iron from her reticule and began to strike the iron against the flint.

The flint took far longer to spark than it should have, largely because her hands were so wet the flint and iron kept slipping from her fingers. But eventually, she was able to catch a few sparks on a handful of leaves, which were devoured immediately. By the time they were all eaten, though, the sticks had caught as well. And though it made her wet all over again, Gisele was able to snag a number of damp sticks from beneath the trees. After arranging them around the fire to dry, she removed her soaking cloak and laid it over a large boulder before settling in to enjoy the fire's warmth and light.

"They're a pitiful bunch of flames if I ever saw any," she said to the birds, who were busy shaking themselves dry. "I would dry you if I had anything dry of my own. I can only guess your wings are too waterlogged to fly," she said. So instead of drying them, she took another handful of leaves and made a little nest for the birds on their rock. Then she built a pile of her own beside the birds' rock and settled into it. Once she was settled in, she looked in her reticule once more. She expected to find nothing else that was useful, but to her surprise, she found something else.

"Oh! But look at this! I do have something dry." Somehow, the cheesecloth that had wrapped her midday meal had stayed dry beneath her cloak. She unfolded it and pulled out the piece of cheese she had meant to eat on the way home. "Here," she said, pulling a few crumbles off and putting them out before the birds. "This is all I have, but you're welcome to it."

The little birds, which had been shaking out their feathers, hopped toward the crumbs and tilted their heads this way, then that. Then the smallest fellow stretched his neck out and nibbled a piece. The others immediately followed, looking expectantly at Gisele when they were done.

"Greedy," she said, laughing as she broke off a few more pieces. "You're far more grateful than my stepsister, though. And far sweeter, too." She smirked. "You also refrain from calling me homely."

She took a bite of cheese and leaned against their rock to watch them squabble over the last piece.

"You know, it's funny. I think this is the idlest I've been in a while." The smallest bird stopped chirping at the others and hopped over to where Gisele leaned her head. "Not that I mind the work. I don't. My parents always worked hard."

The little bird chirped.

"That's easy," she said, daring to reach out and rub the little bird's back with her finger. To her surprise, he didn't hop away. "As I said, I don't mind the work. But I'm..."

What was she? What was it about this errand that hurt so much?

"I suppose," she said slowly, "I'm tired of being invisible."

The third bird, who seemed to have grown bored of looking for cheese crumbs, joined his siblings. Then he chirped as well. It was a lower, throatier sound, which Gisele thought lovely.

"It wasn't always this way. When Mother was alive, our family was whole and happy. But when she died..." The corners of Gisele's eyes stung, and her throat grew tight. "When she died, my father changed. It was as if her death broke something inside of him. And I think...I think he wishes to forget me so he doesn't have to remember..."

A lump rose in Gisele's throat, and she closed her eyes as she tried to force it down. For a long time, there was nothing but the sound of rain pounding outside the cave, the crackle of the tiny fire, and the little chirps the birds let out as they explored their rock and then the ground around them. Eventually, though, Gisele felt the slightest warmth on her hand.

She looked down to realize that the smallest bird had flown the short distance from the stone to her hand and was gazing up at her expectantly.

"Won't let me get away with leaving it off at that, will you?" she asked in a husky voice, wiping the corners of her eyes. Then she sat up and lifted him so that he was at eye level. "Well, I gave it a lot of thought last night, but I still wasn't sure. After today, though, my mind is made up." Her voice grew stronger with each word, as did her conviction. "Becca was right. I don't know what Adrienne has in store for me, but I don't trust her. Nor can I trust my father to protect me the way I once thought he would." She cleared her throat and forced a tremulous smile. "I don't know how. But I'm going to escape this place the first chance I get. Because I have this sense that it's going to get much worse if I don't."

FOUR

Gisele eventually warmed enough that she was able to fall into a light doze. Not deep enough to let the fire go out. That could be fatal. The spring days might be warm, but the nights were still cold, and letting the fire die could easily mean that she might never wake up. Still, after searching the cave once more to find a relatively impressive amount of fuel, she felt safe enough to close her eyes, even if only for a little bit. The sound of the rain and fire combined was soothing, and the angsty energy that had kept her strong during her search for the axe and then for shelter was now gone.

What she didn't expect was to hear such realistic voices from her dreams.

"Mummy! Mummy, you found us!" cried a young voice, though Gisele couldn't tell if it belonged to a boy or a girl.

"Of course, I found you, silly thing." This voice was definitely that of a woman. "Now, whatever are you doing all the way over here? And in a cave with a human?"

"She saved us, Mummy!" cried another voice, this one older and more masculine. "We were looking for worms when the rain came, and the only place we could find to hide was under a big tree."

"Why didn't you fly away? Our nest isn't far."

"Our wings were too wet," said a sad little girl's voice. "But the human woman took us into her dress, then she brought us here and made a fire and shared her food!"

This was the strangest dream Gisele had ever had. But she was too tired to rouse herself, so she simply continued to listen to her dream.

"Oh!" the woman's voice replied. She was quiet for a moment. "Did she say why she saved you?"

"No," said the older boy's voice. "But she talked to us. A lot."

"Gracious! Did she expect you to talk back?" The mother sounded quite alarmed.

"I don't think so," said the girl slowly. "But I do think she's lonely."

"Yeah," said the little one. "And she says we're nicer than her stepsister. And we don't call her homely."

"Why would we call her homely?" the oldest asked. "And what does homely mean?"

"It's a cruel thing to call someone," said the mother sharply.

"That would make sense," the girl said with a sigh. "She doesn't seem very happy."

The mother was quiet for a long time. So quiet that Gisele was wondering if she had changed dreams when the mother finally spoke again.

"The rain will end soon. And I have something I must discuss with the others."

AFTER THAT, Gisele's dreams really did change, and in what seemed like a moment later, the world around her was light, and Gisele blinked her eyes open to find that the sky was clear, and brilliant golden sunlight had flooded the world outside the cave.

Though she was still damp, she had indeed dried far more than she'd expected with such small flames. She turned to see how the little birds were doing when she realized they were gone.

"Birds?" she called, getting on her knees to examine the cave around her. "Little birds?"

It was quite silly, really, looking for the little birds. The storm seemed long over, and they had most likely flown away as soon as the sky was clear. But for some reason, this made her sad. Until she heard chirping from above.

"Birds?" Gisele looked up, but there was nothing there. Except...she paused and realized she felt a slight pressure on her head. Reaching up, she found...

Were those leaves?

Slowly, she removed whatever was on her head to examine it. Then she let out a small cry of delight.

Someone had placed a small wreath of white and pink rosebuds along with their verdant leaves on her head. And when she peeked beneath the flower petals, she found three tiny birds sitting inside. When she saw them, they began to sing.

"Oh!" Gisele stared at the birds. As she watched them, their song grew even louder. "I...I suppose..." She didn't know what to suppose. Last night, she had saved three little birds. Then she dreamed about those little birds finding their mother bird. And now, she was wearing the most beautiful wreath of roses she had ever seen, and the little birds hidden inside of it seemed to be singing to her.

"Well," she said to the little birds, "if my mother ever taught me anything, it was never to take a faerie gift for granted. And you, my loves, are definitely a faerie gift or something of the sort." Though she felt a little silly putting a wreath of small birds on her head, she put the wreath back on at once. The faerie would most likely be watching some-where nearby. And it would never do to make the faerie think she disliked her gift. Her life was difficult enough with her stepmother in it. The last thing Gisele needed was an angry faerie as well.

Gisele gathered her father's axe and her cloak, which had dried enough to don it again, stomped out the remaining embers of the fire, and made her way to a nearby pond, where she could get a better look at her gift. Holding onto the wreath so it wouldn't slip off, she bent over the water to peer at her reflection.

It really was a beautiful wreath. And though it might be childish to admit it, wearing the roses made her feel like a princess. She stood and searched the countryside around her. Nearby were the woods she'd stumbled through last night, the cave, and behind her were fields and fields of perfectly laid rows of sprouts.

"Thank you!" she called out, her voice seeming oddly loud in the still air. "The wreath is beautiful, and I shall wear it with pride. And...whenever the little birds wish to go, I will let them." She had no idea whether or not this was the proper way to address a faerie, as she had never addressed one before, but as she wasn't blasted with a curse, she decided to assume it would do. So she picked up her father's axe again and started home.

IF THE ROSES made Gisele feel pretty, the birds and their constant songs made her feel as though she had companions, and by the time she arrived back at her father's house, she felt far happier than she had felt in days.

"Gisele?" her father called out when she closed the door behind her. Gisele hesitated. The thought of hiding in the barn for a few more hours was enticing. She could avoid her stepmother and stepsister, *and* take another doze in the warm hay. But the anxiety in her father's voice bade her continue to the kitchen, even though she wondered deep down if it might not do him some good to worry about her for a while longer.

The scene she entered in the kitchen was a cozy one. Her stepmother was cutting bread, and her stepsister was sipping tea from the side of the table that was nearest the window. Her father was seated in a chair on the opposite side of the table, his ankle wrapped in what looked like yards of cloth.

"You're back!" he exclaimed, hobbling to his feet when she walked in. "What happened?"

"Did you get the axe head?" Adrienne asked, not looking up from the bread she was slicing.

"I got caught in the storm," Gisele said, ignoring her stepmother's question. She shouldn't have been surprised that Adrienne's first concern was for the tool that kept their income. But she was, nonetheless.

"Caught in the storm?" her father asked incredulously. "But where did you stay?"

"Did you–" Adrienne began again, finally looking up from her knife, but she was interrupted by Simone,

"What is *that* on your head?"

Before Gisele could answer, though, Adrienne put down her knife and stalked over to Gisele. Gisele took an instinctive step back, but her stepmother followed, continuing to study her wreath.

"Did you make this?" she snapped.

Gisele put her right hand up to touch the leaves. "No."

"Then what foolishness is this?" Adrienne snapped, grabbing the wreath and yanking it off Gisele's head.

"What are you doing?" Gisele cried, but it was too late. The roses shriveled and faded, and the leaves turned brown. The little birds who had stopped singing at Adrienne's touch flew out, their chirps now little cries of alarm, before flying out the nearest open window.

"What did you do that for?" Gisele turned back to her stepmother.

"I'm trying to get your sister married, and you're parading about in stupid frivolities like this, as if you can't bear to let her have the attention!" Adrienne snapped.

Gisele opened her mouth to tell her stepmother just what she thought of her behavior, but her father's voice boomed through the kitchen.

"Adrienne!"

All three women turned to stare at him, and for the first time, Gisele saw a flicker of fear in her stepmother's face. Gisele's father had never spoken to her like that before.

"I don't know what fool things they teach you up in town, but anyone who's lived in the country for an hour would recognize that as a gift of the faerie!" Gisele's father continued.

Adrienne scoffed and threw the broken wreath on the ground. "A gift of the faerie—"

"I thought I married a woman of sense!" Gisele's father continued. "But if you're too stupid to recognize faerie magic when you see it, then this house is no place for you. Or your progeny!"

Though his anger wasn't directed in the way Gisele had hoped—namely that Adrienne had forced Gisele to spend the night in the woods during a storm—she did feel satisfaction warm her middle as Adrienne—for once—looked as though she had nothing to say.

"Now," Gisele's father said, "I let you use this house for whatever you can imagine. I let you parade her around," he waved his hand at Simone, "so men of all sorts can come calling, interrupting work five times a day it seems."

"Now dear," Adrienne said, blinking rapidly, "that's not exactly fair–"

"But invite danger into my home by abusing gifts of magic, and you'll find you and your daughter out on the street where I found you!"

While this wasn't exactly true, as Adrienne had never lived on the street after her first husband's death, Adrienne seemed to finally grasp that he was telling the truth. She closed her mouth and gave her husband an overly sweet smile.

"Of course, darling. My apologies." She turned to Gisele. "I'm sorry your gift is torn." Then she went back to the table and began slicing the bread once again.

"Gisele," she said in that same sickly sweet voice, "tell us how you received such a gift."

Gisele had no desire to tell her stepmother anything. But as her father was watching her, she sighed and related the tale of the storm, and the little birds, and the cave, and the dream.

Though she had felt most satisfied at watching her father finally put his awful wife in place for once, the sweetness of victory was quickly gone, and Gisele was left with a bitter taste in her mouth. Already she missed her little friends, and her head felt naked without the comforting pressure of the flowers.

For the rest of the meal, Gisele was treated with more courtesy than she had been since the marriage. And it made her suspicious.

"Well," her father said after he finished his food, "I'm

going back to finish splitting the wood." He turned to Gisele. "Would you like to go with me? Or are you too tired?"

"Oh, let her stay and rest today," Adrienne hurried to say, putting her hands on Gisele's shoulders. "She's had a difficult time." Then she smiled broadly. "Take Simone instead."

The whole kitchen seemed to freeze in time.

"You want her...to come with me?" Gisele's father asked.

"You want me to do what?" Simone cried at the same time.

"Yes," Adrienne said, still smiling too broadly. "You were just saying the other day that Gisele works so hard. And she does! So I think you should take Simone instead."

Simone did *not* want to help her stepfather split wood. But Adrienne was firm, and eventually, Gisele's stepsister followed Gisele's father out into the sunlight with her parasol, grumbling every step of the way.

Gisele half-expected her stepmother to turn on her the moment they were out of sight. But to her surprise, Adrienne simply smiled at her.

"Go rest, dear. You've earned it."

Whatever her stepmother was plotting, Gisele wanted no part of it. But she was also exhausted, so she was more than happy to leave her stepmother to her own devices and hide in her room alone. But after changing into her nightdress and snuggling up in her bed, Gisele heard Becca's words echo in her head.

Adrienne was definitely up to no good.

Adrienne hadn't been wrong. Gisele *was* exhausted from her night in the cave, but she was unable to sleep more than a few hours at a time, largely because she continued startling awake, wondering what Adrienne was up to while she slept. But every time she checked, her stepmother was busy doing some sort of innocuous chore. She did, however, look far too smug for Gisele's comfort.

Finally, halfway through the afternoon, Gisele gave up on sleep and got up, washed her face, brushed her hair, and went to the barn to care for the animals. And as she worked, she wondered.

Since her father had married Adrienne, no one had dared even suggest Simone accompany her stepfather to his labor the way Gisele did. In fact, while Adrienne had proven herself capable of basic household chores, Simone had never, to Gisele's knowledge, lifted so much as one finger to help. She could not remain in the sun for long, her mother fretted, or her snowy complexion might darken or freckle. Her hands, which were softer than Gisele's had been at the age of eight, ventured to do nothing more taxing than embroidery, and even then, only for short periods of time. She drank honeyed tea for hours every day and slept three hours every afternoon.

Knowing all this, Gisele doubted very much that Adrienne's desire for Simone to accompany her stepfather out into the woods had much to do with a change of heart, and most likely had more to do with some misguided wish for something like the wreath to befall her child. But really, what did she think would happen? Gisele had been working in the woods and fields her whole life, and only now had some faerie seen fit to gift her. And even that was probably out of simple gratitude for Gisele's aiding the little birds. Faeries, as it was well known among the country dwellers, were dearly attached to animals.

Did Adrienne really think such a situation could be replicated?

Her thoughts were interrupted when a tremendous bang erupted from inside the house. Gisele hurried to put away the pitchfork she'd been moving hay with, and ran inside to find her father facing off with Simone, who had something white trickling down her head. The door must have been the source of the noise, for it still stood ajar.

"I have no idea what happened!" her father was shouting. "All I know was that I was splitting wood, and she starts shrieking at the top of her lungs–"

"Then let her get a word in, and maybe we'll find out!"

Adrienne turned to her daughter. "Simone, darling, what happened? What's upset you so?"

"Dirty creatures!" Simone snapped.

"What?" Adrienne blinked.

"Dirty creatures!" Simone shouted more loudly this time.

"I am trying to help you!" Adrienne hissed. "Now if you take that tone again with me–"

"Dirty creatures. Dirty creatures, dirty creatures, dirty creatures!" Simone burst into tears and fled to her room. Gisele, her father, and Adrienne stood staring at one another for a long moment.

"Tell me," Adrienne said in a quivering voice. "Before this happened, what *exactly* did she do?"

Gisele's father shrugged. "I told you, I don't know. She...she sat watching me work for a long time, and she wasn't very happy about it. Then, when I told her we were almost done, she huffed and stomped into the forest, muttering something about silly birds and wreaths." His gaze narrowed. "Did you send her to get a wreath of her own?"

Adrienne sniffed. "So what if I did? Finish your story."

Gisele's father frowned, but he continued. "Anyhow, a little while later, I heard her shriek, so I followed her to see what was wrong. When I found her, she was at the edge of the forest, shooing away some little doves. One looked like it had...uh..."

"Had what?" Adrienne snapped.

Gisele's father blushed slightly. "Relieved itself on her head."

Gisele tried to suppress a snort, but it was too late. After shooting her an icy glare, Adrienne turned back to Gisele's father. "And what happened then?"

"I don't know!" He ran a hand through his dark hair. "One minute, she's shouting about the horrible birds, and the next minute, she's saying just what she said in here. 'Dirty creatures! Dirty creatures!' She's said naught else since then."

Adrienne stared at him, her mouth falling open slightly. Gisele wondered if she ought to quietly slip out, but as soon as she took a step toward the door, Adrienne fixed her with a stare that froze her in place.

Gisele's father licked his lips and spoke again, more slowly this time. "Adrienne, um, what...what was the point in sending Simone with me today? What exactly were you hoping for her to do?"

Adrienne folded her arms. "What's your point?"

"Well, we know this...whatever it is that's gotten hold of Simone isn't something natural. And I can't help but wonder if Simone hasn't gotten on some faerie's bad side."

As soon as the words were out of his mouth, Gisele knew he was right. The little birds. The strange words. Simone's complete lack of knowledge about anything having to do with animals. It all made sense. Most likely, whatever faerie had fashioned the wreath for Gisele–to reward her for her kindness to the birds–had seen it fit to fashion a curse for her stepsister after Simone had somehow offended the being's beloved birds.

Adrienne looked for a moment as though she might murder her husband. But then she drew in a long, deep breath and spoke again with surprising calm. "Well, whatever it was, I'll get it fixed." She glowered at Gisele. "No matter *what* the cost."

What was that supposed to mean?

"Pierre," Adrienne turned back to her husband, "I'll need the cart and horse tomorrow."

"That cart? What for?" he asked.

"To see my godmother!" she hissed. "What is it to you?"

"I'm supposed to make it to the regional market tomorrow, remember? I have a buyer for some of the extra wood. Wait, you have a godmother?"

In spite of herself, Gisele stared at her as well. Adrienne had never mentioned having a godmother.

"Then you can walk. You've been getting round enough in the middle that it will do you some good. And yes, I have a godmother. I don't like to shout it from the streets, but–"

A knock sounded at the door. Adrienne's face turned ashen. "Master Gilead!" she whispered.

Master Gilead was Simone's beau.

"Pierre, you must stall him while I help Simone!" Adrienne said quickly. "Keep him busy until I can make her presentable!"

"Just tell him she's ill. It's not a–"

"Just do it!"

Master Gilead was a local lord's son, and Simone had caught his eye about a year prior. Back then, Adrienne's first husband had still been alive, as had Gisele's mother. And though Master Gilead hadn't officially begun to pursue her at that time, their flirtations were legendary, and his admiration of the poverty-stricken beauty was the talk of the town. He hadn't officially begun to court her, however, until after Adrienne and Gisele's father were married.

Gisele had her own opinions on the timing of all this, especially as Adrienne's marriage to her father–a successful woodcutter and respected member of the community–had allowed Master Gilead to officially begin his courtship without besmirching his family's reputation. Her father, however, wasn't interested in hearing them.

Master Gilead had never given Gisele more than a passing glance before. So she found it most entertaining now as he was forced to sit in her presence, accepting her hospitality and making small talk because she found great delight in forcing him to give it.

"I must say, sir," she said as she filled his tea cup. "You've been a most attentive suitor. Simone is enthralled with you."

"As I am with her," Master Gilead said, keeping his focus on his tea. "That's enough honey. Thank you."

"Your attentions are most revealing," Gisele said, keeping her eyes wide and hoping they looked innocent. "Which makes me wonder." She leaned her chin on her hand and tried to look lovestruck. "What is it about her that made you *sure* you wanted to know her more?"

"Gisele!" Gisele's father said sharply, but Gisele simply suppressed a grin as Master Gilead looked everywhere but her.

"It was her...beauty, of course. And her charm."

"She is so wonderfully charming," Gisele said with her best besotted smile. "But tell me, is it her wit? Her intelligence? Or her kind heart that drew you first?"

"Gisele!" her father hissed.

"Yes, Father?" Gisele tried to give him an innocent smile, but she knew her eyes were laughing far too much for that.

Master Gilead fidgeted. "Um, her kindness."

Well, Gisele knew he was lying now. And she nearly pitied him for it. For while Simone was no scholar, she did have a good deal of wit when it meant wielding her tongue like a knife. This young man was in for a very long, miserable life.

Master Gilead was saved from more of her questions as Adrienne and Simone emerged from the hall, beaming as though it might kill them. Simone's hair was damp but free of all remnants of the bird incident, and a scarf was tied delicately around her throat.

"Master Gilead," Adrienne said with a deep curtsey. "Forgive us for making you wait! I will confess that," her face became tragic, "Simone isn't feeling well today. She's caught cold, and her voice is quite gone."

"My darling," Master Gilead was suddenly all warmth and affection as he launched himself from his seat to Simone's side. "Are you well enough to be out of bed?"

"She'll need to return soon, but she wanted so much to see you." Adrienne clasped her hands as Simone allowed herself to be lowered carefully into Master Gilead's chair.

"I...I don't wish to keep you from your recovery," he said, kneeling on the floor beside her, "so I'll do what I came to do." Pulling a ring with a large diamond from his cloak, he held it between them. "My darling Simone."

Simone's eyes had grown to the size of walnuts at the

appearance of the stone, and she looked nowhere else as he continued.

"You are the most beautiful creature in all of the world. I am sure of it. And your heart is just as lovely to match."

Gisele stifled a gag.

"So when I told my mother and sister that I wished to make you mine, they insisted that I bring this, my family's heirloom ring, to ask you–to usher you into joining our family." He paused. "What do you say? Will you marry me?"

Simone, whose eyes had not left the diamond since he had pulled it from his pocket, opened her mouth. And under her mother's horrified stare, whispered two fateful words.

"Dirty creatures."

MASTER GILEAD's admiration for Simone's beauty might have been strong, but his familial pride was stronger. And after Simone insulted his mother and sister not once but twice, he stormed out, declaring that he would never return, and that he had been a fool to ever entertain the thought of marrying a girl of such mean class.

When Adrienne chased him out of the house, begging him to return and hear their explanation, Gisele decided it was within her best interests not to remain in the near vicinity. She slipped back out to the barn and cleaned and tended the animals until she was sure she could safely crawl into her bed without being noticed.

Simone was asleep by the time Gisele snuck in, but she

continued to whimper in her sleep. Gisele expected to hear silence from the room next door, as her father's mornings started before dawn, and Gisele's father and stepmother were usually in bed once the day's work was done. But tonight, they stayed up, talking for hours.

"I told you not to tempt the faeries," Gisele heard her father say reproachfully. "You can't blame this on me."

"You have no...no idea what I've done to get my daughter such a suitor!" Adrienne retorted. "*No* idea."

"She's beautiful enough." Gisele's father sounded bored. "Find her another one."

"It's not that simple, you foolish man! Don't you realize Master Gilead will talk? Before the week's over, every nobleman will know what she said! And no one worth dowry will so much as look at her!"

"Just tell them she's cursed."

"That will make it worse!"

A gentle rain began to fall outside, and its low pitter-patters came through Gisele's slightly open window. Her father and stepmother's voices began to blend together then fade away as Gisele, in desperate need of sleep, began to doze off.

At some point, the rain ended. And at about the same time, a bird began to sing. Then, not long after that, there were new voices to be heard. And none of them belonged to Gisele's family.

"Mummy, wasn't it funny to see the ugly girl scream?" said a young boy. "Oh, look! There she is in bed!"

"Hush. We don't laugh at people's pain. And we don't call them ugly."

"But she was mean!" a young girl's voice said. "She tried to hit Edwin! You said that acting like that makes us ugly!"

"Which is why," the mother's voice hardened, "I cursed her. But that's not why we're here. Quickly, now. I've sung a song that will put them both to sleep, but we need to remake the wreath before they wake up."

Gisele felt that she ought to get up. She ought to see who was talking. And it sounded very much as though they were talking about her and Simone. She was dreaming, though, so the voices couldn't possibly be real. And yet...they sounded so near that she felt as though she might be able to reach out and touch whoever spoke them. For some reason, though, she couldn't rouse herself enough to open her eyes.

"Why are you making it differently this time?" the little girl's voice asked.

"This time, I'm making it so that not only do the flowers and leaves remain fresh, but so that no one can snatch it from her head."

"Like that mean lady did?" the little boy asked. "I saw her do it through the window."

"Precisely. Now, are you sure you want to get in the wreath first? Or would you like your brothers and sisters to take the first turn?"

"Oh, no!" exclaimed the little girl. "We want to go first! They can take their turns later!"

WHEN GISELE WOKE up the next morning, she had the strangest sensation that she should remember something. But before she could discern what it was that she should remember, the sound of baby birds made her look up. And there on her open windowsill lay a new rose wreath.

"Oh!" she breathed, reaching out to stroke one of the rosebuds. When she did, the little birdsong grew even louder. Laughing, Gisele placed the gift on her head.

"You're back, are you?" she said in a low voice. But one glance at the other side of the room told her that Simone was already out of bed. She needn't be afraid of being over-heard. "I missed you, you know."

"Don't forget to have Gisele finish splitting the pile for me. It's nearly done. The axe is in the barn."

"I'll tell her," came her stepmother's voice from the other room. Compared to the night before, it was strangely calm. "Now go. You have a long walk ahead of you."

Her father's low farewell and the following slam of a door signaled that he had left for the regional market. Which meant he would be gone for quite some time. In the old days, he had never been gone for more than three or four nights at most. But these days, whenever he had business dealings to make, he tended to come home less and less. Before Gisele could decide how she might take advantage of his absence, footsteps made their way to her door. Gisele dove under the covers again, careful to put her arm under her head so she didn't damage the wreath or hurt the birds. She closed her eyes and pretended to sleep just before her bedroom door burst open.

Her stepmother's quick steps crossed half of the room

before they stopped. Gisele stayed silent and unmoving for a long moment, hoping she would go away.

And at first, it seemed to work. Adrienne turned around and went back to the kitchen. Gisele stayed still, however, and was wondering if she ought to pretend to wake up when Adrienne returned. And something hard smashed down on Gisele's thigh.

Gisele let out a cry and whipped around, but her step-mother, who was brandishing the broom, only brought the wooden handle down on her leg again.

"Stop!" Gisele cried, throwing her arms around her legs and pressing herself against the wall. "What are you doing?"

"I'm not going to touch the wreath because it seems my foolish husband's superstitions were somehow founded," Adrienne said. "But you should know that I blame *you*." As she said the words, she hit Gisele again.

"I had nothing to do with the curse!" Gisele cried, sticking an arm out in front of her. "I wasn't even there!"

"No, but you were the one who stirred up that ridiculous faerie's interest! If you had just kept to your own business, this never would have happened!"

"But I–"

"A *lord*, Gisele!" Adrienne screamed. "She was being wooed by the son of a *lord*! And once word gets out about this, no man in his right mind will want to marry her!"

Gisele stared at her stepmother. She should try to grab the broomstick. But Adrienne, for all her feminine perfection, was strong and a whole handspan taller than Gisele. Trying to take the weapon might make her use it more.

"Now," Adrienne said, tucking the broom beneath her

arm as though she'd just finished sweeping. "I've gotten your father to leave me the cart for the day. I'm going to take Simone up to my godmother to see what she can do about this curse. In the meantime, I expect the house to be spotless when I return. She turned and walked toward the door. But she paused on the threshold and turned to face Gisele once more, this time, with a small vindictive smile. "And if you wish to tell your father about our little conversation, go ahead. See who he believes."

Gisele sat shaking in her bed for a long time after the sound of the cart rolled away.

More than ever before, she knew now that Becca was right. Adrienne had never been good to Gisele, but never before had she raised her hand against her. And though Gisele hoped her father would believe her, a quiet voice deep down knew that Adrienne was most likely right.

The wreath shivered slightly, then a small familiar white and gray fluffball flew down to land on her finger.

"I'm sorry you had to hear that," Gisele said, her voice still trembling. "But I'm glad you're here."

The little bird began to sing and was soon joined by two other little rounds of chirps from within the wreath. And in spite of her tears, Gisele smiled.

J ulien brought his horse to a stop and looked around. He had been thinking about his mother's exasperated wish that morning that he might learn to one day take life more seriously, but that thought would have to be finished at another time.

For now, he was most definitely lost.

"Where did she send us?" he muttered to his horse. "I don't know where we are, but it isn't the Regional Market."

He'd been following the road for two hours now, half an hour longer than it should have taken him to reach the largest market in the kingdom. He'd been to the market before, of course, but when Mother Dove had promised him that a little side road would be a shortcut, he hadn't stopped to question whether or not she knew what she was doing.

Mother Dove always knew what she was doing.

Which made him wonder all the more what she was up to.

"Perhaps she's punishing me for some new offense," he told his horse. "Now I just need to figure out what I've done this time." His horse only turned his head enough to give him an unimpressed glance.

"Well, there's water over there. We might as well get you a drink." Julien dismounted and led the horse to a bubbling little brook.

Well, if Mother Dove was going to punish him, at least she'd gotten him lost in one of the prettiest places Julien had ever seen. The world around him had exploded into every shade of green imaginable, from the wild grass to the leaves to the pine needles on the evergreens. Flower buds of blue, pink, and yellow were everywhere, and the brook sang happily as it tumbled against the rocks. Young stalks of some sort of new crop were beginning to grow in perfectly ordered fields in the distance, and the sky was an endless blue. As lovely as it all was, though, it still wasn't the Regional Market.

While his horse drank, Julien went back to the road.

"All right!" he called loudly. "Tell me what I've done so I can apologize for it. Then please put me back on the right path!"

There was no answer.

"Mother Dove!" he called out again. "I really do need to meet with Lord Hibbins."

If Mother Dove heard him, she didn't make a sound. With a huff, Julien walked back to his horse and was about to mount him again when a voice caught his attention. It was a woman's voice, and she was singing. He paused to listen, and after some seconds, realized that the woman's voice was accompanied by...were those birds?

Slowly, Julien led his horse through the trees and brush toward the voice. If Mother Dove wasn't going to help him, he might as well get help from someone else.

The sound of an axe on wood echoed through the valley as well, and it seemed to be coming from the same direction as the voice, its loud crack accenting the beats of the song.

Finally, Julien made his way around a particularly large tree to find a young woman standing in a small clearing, splitting small logs on a large wooden stump.

The song she sang was lighthearted and quick, but even more amazing was that a number of birds–which he couldn't see–seemed to be harmonizing with her. The girl wore a common work dress, but on her head was the loveliest wreath of roses he'd ever seen. As intriguing as it was impractical for woodcutting.

The girl straightened and looked around. When she saw him, she dropped a quick curtsey then shouldered her axe, looking somewhat suspicious.

"Can I help you?" she asked, her brow slightly furrowed.

He could only guess that being a young woman all alone in the woods with a stranger would give her reason to be suspicious. He removed his hat and bowed low. "My apologies for interrupting." Hopefully, he hadn't frightened her.

Her sharp gaze traveled up and down his clothing. She had curtsied, so it was likely that she knew he was of higher rank simply due to the cut and quality of his clothes and his horse. But he doubted she knew what he really was, as her curtsey hadn't been particularly deep. He almost smiled to himself. All the better.

"How can I help you?" she asked again.

"I'm loath to say it," he said, grinning sheepishly as he held his hat in his hands. "But I'm afraid I'm lost."

Her brow unfurrowed slightly. "Oh. Well, where are you looking to go?"

"The Regional Market. I was told this road was a shortcut."

"No," she said slowly, frowning again, "I'm afraid you're nowhere near the Regional Market. In fact...where did you come from?"

"The capital city," he said vaguely.

"If that's the case, you've been going in the opposite direction all morning. It's a good eight-hour walk from here." She glanced behind him. "Though, I'm not sure what it would take on a horse."

Julien stared at her then shook his head and laughed.

"What's so funny?" she asked.

He continued to chuckle. "It seems I was given the wrong directions on purpose." Julien wasn't in the habit of taking directions from animals. But Mother Dove wasn't just any animal. And she, more than any, would know whether or not the road she sent him down would be a shortcut. No faerie-blessed animal would make that mistake.

"If you're looking for the right road," the girl said, resting her axe on the stump, "you can cut through my father's field here." She pointed to the south. "Then you'll find a small dusty path that leads up to Shadeling. If you follow Shadeling's main road, you'll reach a fork in the road in about an hour. The road to the right will take you back to the capital city. The one to the left will take you to the market."

"I thank you." He bowed again and turned to his horse. Then he stopped. If Mother Dove had sent him this far, he might as well have a rest. And he had the sudden desire to rest near this pretty girl.

"Would you mind if I rest here for a few moments?" He gestured to his horse. "My horse would like to graze before we begin again."

She studied him for a long moment before nodding. "Very well." Then she bent and grabbed another small log.

He studied her unabashedly as she worked. She wasn't beautiful in the contrived way most noblewomen were. But there was a raw attractiveness to her, a natural pleasantness that made him wish to look more. Her eyes, a pale blue, were bright and sharp, and her long brown hair flowed unfettered down her shoulders and back as though she didn't care what it did. She was of average height and looked slightly underfed, but she was also strong, a strength he guessed that came with cutting wood.

"What's your name?" he asked.

"Gisele," she said before smashing the axe down on a piece of log. A long crack formed down the center. Then she straightened and wiped her forehead with her arm. "And who, might I ask, are you?"

Julien laughed without thinking. Her eyes widened

slightly when he started laughing, but that only made it all the more humorous. She was bold, this little woodcutter. Most young women saw the quality of his clothes and either burst into simpering giggles or seductive charms. This girl, while polite, seemed to have neither time nor interest in either of those reactions. She really seemed to have no idea who he was.

"Emile," he said. It wasn't a lie. Emile was his second name.

The girl–Gisele–nodded politely. "It is good to meet you, Emile." Then she went back to her cutting.

Julien watched her a moment longer before standing and taking the axe from her.

"Excuse me, sir!" she stared up at him indignantly. "What do you think you're doing?"

"I'm going to split logs for a bit, and you're going to sit and eat."

She stared at him as if he'd grown horns. "You're going to...what?"

"What I just said. I'll cut. You eat."

She flushed slightly. "I haven't anything to eat." Then she raised her chin. "And pardon the assumption, but what would a fine young gentleman such as yourself know of chopping wood?"

Julien raised one eyebrow, and took a larger piece of wood from the pile. Then he placed it on the stump upon which she'd been cutting and raised the axe above his head. Gisele hurried backward as he brought it crashing down, the two halves of the wood flying in opposite directions.

The look she gave him made him privately determine to

thank his swordmaster when he got home. The man had forced him to chop wood to strengthen his shoulders when he was young. As a thirteen-year-old boy, he'd resented it with every fiber of his being. He had wanted to learn swords, and wood cutting was a skill he'd been sure would waste away forever. Clearly, his thirteen-year-old self had been mistaken.

"Well," Gisele said, clearing her throat slightly. "I...judged wrongly."

Julien smirked then nodded at his horse. "If you look in the saddlebags on the left side, you'll find more than enough food for both of us. Take it out and eat as much as you want while I do this."

The girl seemed hesitant to agree, but eventually, the invisible birds began to twitter anxiously. As if in a dream, she slowly turned and did as he said.

A few minutes later, a vast spread of food was laid out on a large rock nearby, and she was staring at it as though she wasn't sure what to do.

He grabbed another log. "If you don't mind me asking, why don't you have any food?" It was a rather intrusive question and probably impolite. But, Julien argued with himself, what good was having power if you couldn't use it to learn how your people fared? He'd been to the village she'd mentioned–Shadeline–only a few days before, and the people had seemed well-fed enough. Unless there was another crop blight he was unaware of. If so, he would need to alert his father.

"My...stepmother sent me none," she said hesitantly, gazing longingly at the food.

Julien paused long enough to grab an apple and take a bite before putting it back down and taking another log. "Eat. Then tell me why your stepmother sent you no food." As the words came out of his mouth, he realized how commanding they sounded. Of course, that was how he spoke and was expected to speak at home. But out here, it just sounded overbearing.

Gisele frowned up at him slightly, seeming to think the same thing, when three little birds flew out of her wreath and began pecking at her hands.

"Fine! Fine!" she said, gently shooing at them with her hands. "I'll eat! But it's your fault if I get poisoned." Seeming satisfied, the little birds flew back up to her wreath and immediately nestled into it again.

Julien realized he was staring and forced himself to focus on the wood. He was getting more and more curious about this girl. But he'd better stick with one topic of conversation at a time.

"Is your family struggling?" he asked gently.

Gisele hesitated slightly before taking a small bite of bread. The way she briefly closed her eyes and sighed told him how hungry she really was. Then she opened her eyes and shrugged. "I offended her."

He stopped cutting. "So she gave you no food?" Cutting was hard work. Already, he was being reminded of how long it had been since his swordmaster had made him cut, and he liked to think himself in excellent health and strength. This girl was two heads shorter than he was and weighed far less. He couldn't imagine how hungry she must be after a full morning of such work.

Gisele kept her eyes on the bread. "My father is away." As if that explained it.

He put the axe down. "And will you tell your father when he returns?"

"I will, but I don't think he'll choose to hear."

Julien continued to study her, anger beginning to swirl in the pit of his stomach. He didn't know the girl well, of course. But if what she said was true–and he saw no reason to doubt her–Gisele was in a terrible situation.

Could he help her?

He could help her, of course, by ordering soldiers to haul the family away for mistreating her so. But then what would be left for her? The life of a lone, unwed woman was difficult and dangerous. He could give her a job in his home, of course, but...was that what she really wanted? To become a servant?

He decided he should get to know her first before he foisted his good intentions onto her without her permission. Her first inclination to his proffered help always seemed to be withdrawal. She was obviously quite self-reliant, and probably with good reason. Push too hard, and he could easily scare her away.

"I have another question," he said, trying to sound casual again. "Where did you get that wreath?"

She froze briefly, but before she could speak, the little birds within it began to tweet as though they were shouting. Gisele glanced up, then gave him a wry smile.

"Very well. I'll tell you. But only if you eat, too."

As his stomach was growling, he stuck the axe into the stump, then joined her on the large, flat rock. As they ate, she told him about her night in the storm and how she couldn't be sure, but she thought she'd dreamed about the voices of birds. Then, when she'd awakened, she was wearing this flower wreath, and now wherever she went, the birds went, too.

From the way she hesitated several times during the retelling, Julien got the feeling that she wasn't telling him everything. The way her family had treated her during the storm was even more reprehensible than not sending her food, and it made him wonder what other awful things they had done to her. But as soon as she began to describe the mother bird's words in her dream, Julien nearly laughed out loud. His strange morning suddenly made sense.

Mother Dove had wanted him to meet Gisele.

Julien's history with Mother Dove was a long one. And it had begun the day he'd climbed a tree and tried to take a few eggs to show his mother. They had been blue and speckled and very beautiful. But before he'd even lifted the eggs from the nest, a very angry, very strong dove had begun to peck at him. Instead of squawking at him as she should have, however, she accompanied her pecks with a steady stream of human rebukes. He'd nearly knocked the nest in sheer terror when she first shouted at him. In fact, her scolding was so thorough that it had ended with him in tears and promising never to steal eggs from nests again.

As he had learned later, Mother Dove was a faerie-blessed bird who had been given dominion and oversight over all the wild birds in the area. She could communicate with human, bird, and beast, and had even been gifted with a limited amount of magic, though she swore it was nowhere near what a real faerie could wield.

After their first encounter, it had seemed she would wait for the young Julien to come outside so she could continue her lecture on the evils of stealing an animal's children and all sorts of other follies she was sure he participated in. For a while, he had dreaded going outside at all. But eventually, he came to realize that she had ceased pecking at him a long time ago, and had been instead imparting wise advice of all sorts. And now, at the age of twenty-three, he trusted her implicitly.

If Mother Dove had gifted this girl a magical wreath that housed her children, she must think highly of her indeed. And that said far more about Gisele's character than any girl Julien had ever met at home or abroad.

"I am most sorry," he said after they finished eating and her story was through, "but I must return to the road. That is, the right road."

"Of course," Gisele said, helping him gather the cloths the food had been wrapped in. "And...thank you. For the company. And the food. And the help." She gave him a small, shy smile.

He packed his saddlebags once more but then paused. This was a girl worth knowing. Mother Dove had certainly believed so, believed it enough to derail his entire day. And now he was sure of it as well.

"Will...will you be back here tomorrow?" he asked hesitantly.

She gestured to the large pile of uncut wood piled

behind her. "I'll be in the area. My father won't be back for days."

He mounted his horse and grinned. "Well, then. Until tomorrow."

"Why?" She quirked one brow. "Are you planning on getting lost again?"

He laughed as he turned his horse. "I just might."

SEVEN

Gisele stayed out as late as she dared before returning to the house. And while she was still annoyed with her father for taking an extended absence, she was grateful for the excuse to linger in the barn doing his chores. Emile's meal had been better than any food she'd ever eaten, and she'd discovered after he'd packed up and gone that he'd left the remainder of his bread wrapped neatly on the rock upon which they'd eaten. This gift meant she could hide outside until it was time to sneak into bed.

She smiled as she hung up her axe and grabbed the pitchfork to muck the dirty hay out of the animal stalls. Her encounter with the young stranger today had been...well, strange. That he would get so completely lost as to ride in the wrong direction for hours would have struck her as suspicious, except that he had seemed genuinely perplexed. And the way he'd let her rest while sharing his food with her...

She should be wary, and she probably shouldn't have eaten his food at all. But after having only an old apple to eat that morning, her stomach had begun aching badly by the time he'd arrived. The aroma coming from his bag of food, not to mention the sight of him shouldering her axe, had been enough to overcome her good sense. He'd treated her as though she were a noble lady, though she had probably looked anything but, and for as long as she could remember, no man had ever done that before. Why he had, she still couldn't say. Whenever she cut wood, her sweat made her clothes sick to her skin, and she was sure she had smudges of dirt everywhere. Still, he'd offered, and she'd been unable to resist.

Besides, watching his shoulders as he split the wood? That had been enough to make her blush. Hopefully, he hadn't seen. She also hoped he'd missed the way she'd studied him as he worked.

Her first assumption that he was a useless noble had been far from correct. And though she'd thought him handsome at first sight, his chivalry had given her a far better advantage from which to admire him.

His hair had varying shades from dark brown all the way to gold, and though it was slightly mussed from the wind, it appeared to have been brushed with care at some point that morning. His sharp eyes were green and mischievous, but not like Adrienne and Simone's green. His were more natural, the color of the flora on the forest floor. He was taller than her father, and while his arms weren't nearly as muscular—probably because he didn't spend all day cutting wood—his whole physique seemed carefully honed as though he could be ready for anything.

Gisele wasn't a man-chaser. She knew her place in the world, and she had no patience for angling after the attention of fools. But for the first time since her mother's death, her heart had quickened, and it had continued to do so at the thought of him since.

Which was quite foolish of her. She'd never had a serious suitor, and this man surely wasn't going to become one now. Her mother had assured her as a girl that she wouldn't have trouble finding a husband one day. "You're beautiful and healthy, and you have a cartload of common sense. Any man who passed you by would be a fool, and you wouldn't want him."

But that had been before Simone had moved in, and Gisele had faded into the background.

Not that Gisele envied Simone's otherworldly beauty, largely because she knew Becca was right. There was something...unsettling about it, though Gisele couldn't name that oddity for what it was. She was vividly aware, however, that no man had ever paid her the attention that Emile had today.

"And no, I'm not delusional enough to think he was doing anything more than flirting," Gisele told the birds as she began putting feed into the animal troughs. "But...it was nice. To be noticed."

The birds stopped singing and twittered at her angrily, but Gisele just smiled and pretended she couldn't understand them. She wasn't finished with her daydream.

Whoever he was—a lord's son, most likely, or possibly even that of an earl—he had noticed. He'd noticed so much, it seemed, that he wished to return. Well, she would believe that when she saw it. Unmarried men, her mother had warned her, were likely to make all sorts of promises to girls that they had no intention of keeping. She would simply have to wait and see.

Still. She had enjoyed—

"Gisele!"

Gisele was so startled by her stepmother's voice that she dropped the bucket of feed she was carrying. The heads of grain scattered all over the floor, only making her stepmother's scowl deepen.

"What are you doing?"

"Feeding the animals," Gisele said blankly. "Since Father's gone—"

"You've been feeding them for two hours. Get in here. I need you."

Gisele frowned at her stepmother's retreating backside, but she followed.

"Dirty creatures," Simone said sullenly as Gisele entered the kitchen.

Gisele's stepsister, it seemed, hadn't had the lovely day Gisele had enjoyed. Their visit to the godmother, whoever she was, must not have been successful, but Gisele knew better than to say this out loud.

"She means for you to get the bed warming stones," Adrienne snapped. "She can't go to bed without them."

"Can't she get her own?" Gisele asked.

Adrienne's gaze narrowed. "Get. The stones. Before I—"

"I'm getting them," Gisele said with a sigh. Maybe if she

did what Adrienne wanted, she would be left alone and allowed to go to bed.

Adrienne, however, had more chores for Gisele than Gisele would have believed possible. Chores, Gisele noticed, that Adrienne usually completed herself. She had no doubt that this was Adrienne's way of punishing her for receiving the wreath, but tonight, Adrienne couldn't keep Gisele's spirits down. For even as Gisele finally lay down to sleep, she was still smiling. And as she began to drift into unconsciousness, she found herself boldly...stupidly hoping Emile would come again.

EMILE DIDN'T COME the next day. Nor the next. By the third day, Gisele's mood was nearly as bad as her stepmother's.

"It's not as though I expected it," she huffed as she brought the axe head down on the wood. "It's the principle of the thing."

The birds continued to chirp away happily as though nothing was wrong, and Gisele wasn't a perpetual stormcloud. And though she loved her little birds, Gisele found herself less than thrilled with their cheerful songs this morning.

"He could have simply enjoyed a nice meal and gone on his way," she continued. "He didn't have to make any promises. I didn't *ask* him to come back."

Finally, after several hours of muttering to herself and the birds as she cut, Gisele put the axe down and made her way to the little nearby brook. She was sipping water from her cupped hands when a horse whinnied to her left.

"There you are!" said a familiar voice.

Gisele looked up to find the handsome stranger standing beside his horse, beaming down at her.

Gisele glared back. He *would* choose to come when her face was wet, and her hair was sticking out every which way. With as much dignity as she could muster, she stood carefully and smoothed her dress, then her hair.

"Lost again?" she asked coldly.

He gave her a sheepish smile, which was annoyingly adorable. "I am sorry about that. My father had a number of tasks for me to finish, and I wasn't able to escape until this morning. I couldn't afford to get lost until they were all done." His smile was still embarrassed, but his green eyes sparkled.

Oh.

Gisele blinked at him. His explanation, much to her annoyance, didn't fit nicely into the story she'd been concocting in her head, one where he rode around wooing young maidens, then never seeing them again. Instead, it made perfect sense. He was young enough not to have full reign of his own time, after all. If he was telling the truth, she would have to forgive him. But she wasn't ready to jump to that point.

Yet.

"And what kind of tasks did you need to accomplish for your father?" she asked, doing her very best to sound politely uninterested as she started walking again.

"More than I'd expected," he said as he followed her.

When they arrived, he removed an axe from one of his saddlebags and joined her. "We learned a few days ago that the local poultry population has been hit by some sort of sickness. It's killed a large portion of the local chickens, and we had to talk to neighboring regions about purchasing more."

"Oh." Gisele hadn't expected that either. It showed a depth of knowledge many local lord's sons didn't have. "I'm familiar with it," she admitted slowly. "We lost three of our hens to it three weeks ago."

"I'm sorry to hear that." He went over to the pile of uncut logs and carried back a large stack. Once again, Gisele was unable to ignore the way the muscles in his back flexed as he did.

"After that, we had several boundary disputes to settle and a meeting about..." He paused and glanced at her. "Well, things I'm sure you wouldn't be interested in. I nearly fell asleep twice, and I was leading the discussion."

Gisele studied him as he loaded another log onto the stump beside hers. If he was telling the truth, she certainly couldn't accuse him of lazing about like many of the local lords' sons.

"Is your stepmother still upset with you?" he asked, his gaze narrowing slightly.

Gisele shrugged. "She's rarely not upset with me, but I'm afraid this offense will last longer than most."

He frowned at her, the angles of his face seeming to sharpen as he did. And Gisele suddenly got the feeling that while he could be warm and playful, Emile was not one to be trifled with. It sent a shiver down her spine.

Their gazes locked for an eternal moment, Gisele watching as he seemed to war with himself about something. What was he thinking? Did it really anger him that her stepmother was treating her poorly? And if it did...

Why?

Whatever the reason, the dark cloud that had been overshadowing his good humor seemed to pass, and he put the axe down and returned to his horse. "Well, in that case, I'll just have to keep getting lost." He returned with an even larger pack of food than he had brought the first time, and Gisele's face flushed as she realized that he must have asked whoever prepared his food to pack more.

This time, instead of working as she ate, he ate alongside her. And though her good sense resisted, she found herself more and more intrigued. And not only that, but she wanted more.

Gisele didn't believe in love at first sight. That was the stuff of tales. The closest she'd ever seen to that myth had been in cases where men were struck senseless by Simone's beauty or when women discovered how much gold or land a young man was really worth. That wasn't love, and neither was what she felt for Emile.

But she was enjoying herself immensely.

How long had it been since she had talked and teased for the fun of it? Rare were the days now when she got to visit her friends in the village, and even rarer were the times when she was free of her family and their wishes. Here and now, however, for this brief moment in time, there was no one to judge her or rebuke her for her impertinence.

Emile was impertinent enough for both of them, and he

was nosy as well. Despite his antics, however, he was a good listener, and though he was often nosy, his questions were deep and thoughtful.

"What is that?" Gisele asked suddenly, looking at his chest. He had undone the top three buttons as he worked, and as he reclined to eat, something gold had flashed from beneath.

Emile looked down. "Oh," he said in a slightly subdued tone. "You saw that, did you?"

"Was I not supposed to?"

He chuckled. "Technically not. But as you don't seem intent on abducting or ransoming me, I'll tell you."

"I don't know." Gisele leaned back. "I am rather handy with an axe."

Emile laughed again. "I'll keep that in mind." He slid a ribbon from around his neck. It had been hidden so well that Gisele hadn't noticed it before. On the end of the ribbon hung a gold medallion about as wide as a plum.

"It's a wish," he said, holding it out for her to see. "I was gifted it by a faerie at birth."

"It's beautiful," Gisele said, leaning forward to study the intricately engraved vines and berries that encircled the center, into which were carved many names.

"My parents kept it for me until I was nineteen," he said, tucking it back into his shirt. "Then they gave it to me to use as I see fit. Although," his eyes brightened again, "you can't *imagine* the number of lectures I've endured on using it wisely."

"So...it means you can make a wish? For anything?" Gisele asked.

"There are stipulations. The usual, of course. I can't make someone agree to love me, nor can I bring anyone who's dead back to life. And I haven't asked, but I'm rather sure I can't use it to ask for more wishes."

"It's wise to keep it hidden," Gisele said, taking a thin slice of cheese. "I can only guess many would love to steal it."

"I'm technically the only one who can use it," Emile said, buttoning his shirt back up. "But yes, I thought it wise to keep it quiet." Then his eyes sparkled as he leaned forward. "Mostly, I use it to threaten my family."

Gisele frowned at him. "That's terrible."

Emile laughed even more. "You should see the looks on their faces when I say I might wish for a solid gold statue of a mongoose. Or a naked cat, one of those really ugly bald, wrinkled ones. Or to change the law to allow me five wives."

"Emile!" Gisele began, but she was cut off by his roar of laughter. Emile was doubled over, laughing so hard he could barely breathe.

"That's the look my mother gives me!"

And as if she finally remembered how, Gisele laughed too.

EIGHT

A bright light shone in Gisele's face. She groaned and blinked, trying to roll over and escape its shine.

"You're not going to cut wood today," Adrienne announced loudly, holding her candle closer still to Gisele's eyes. Gisele blinked rapidly and tried shoving her stepmother's arm away.

"Do you have to blind me to tell me that?"

"Don't be impertinent. Now get up and wash your face. You're going to my godmother's house. I need you to pick up some beeswax for Simone. My godmother hopes it will break the curse. And tell those stupid birds to shut up."

At the mention of Adrienne's godmother, Gisele went still. For some reason, her new errand sent a chill down her back, but her head was still too muddled from sleep to say exactly why. She pulled the covers back up to her chest and tried to soak up their warmth.

"Your godmother's house?"

"Yes, yes. I'll give you instructions, but you've seen it a million times. You won't be able to miss it."

Gisele wanted badly to point out that nothing was wrong with Simone's feet, and she could walk there as easily as Gisele. Gisele wanted to be at the clearing in case Emile came again. He had said he would try. But something made her hold her tongue. If she argued, Adrienne would argue back. And whenever Adrienne talked, she issued orders. Gisele wanted as few of those as possible.

Before leaving, she snuck out to the barn and gathered the extra eggs from her hens before wrapping them carefully in a straw-filled basket. Then she stole silently outside in the hopes that her stepmother wouldn't know she was gone until Gisele was too far away to hear.

Once she was sure she was out of shouting range from the cottage, Gisele ran the rest of the way to the clearing, and with a stick, scratched what she hoped looked like a village on the big rock. If Emile showed up, hopefully, he would know where she went and that she hadn't aban-doned him. Once that was done, she made her way to town.

The market was bustling by the time she arrived, the sun already high and warm in the sky. The varied smells of food, animals, and dirt filled the air, and though their mixture didn't make a particularly pleasing one, Gisele breathed it in deeply, reveling in another short bout of freedom.

"Gisele!"

Gisele looked over to find April waving at her from her family's vegetable market stand. Gisele smiled and went to join her friend. "You're just who I was looking for," she said after giving April a hug.

"What are you doing in town?" April asked. "I thought your stepmonster couldn't leave your father's land during the week."

Gisele gave her friend a wry smile. "I'm on an errand to fetch something from her godmother."

April's eyes grew wide. "She has a godmother?"

Gisele shrugged. "Apparently, she does. Though what kind of woman could be godmother to Adrienne isn't one I'm particularly excited about meeting."

Actually, Gisele was quite apprehensive. The very idea that Adrienne believed her godmother could undo a faerie curse was disconcerting. But Gisele wasn't about to tell her friend that and worry her more.

"She's using you like her personal servant," April said with a frown. "Mother–"

"Will worry herself to death if you keep telling her the things I tell you." Gisele put her basket on the table. "Oh, but I did want to know if you could try to sell these for me."

April peeked inside the basket. "Eggs!" She looked back up at Gisele. "These will sell for a high price right now."

"Keep half for yourself and give me the other half the next time I see you," Gisele said.

"I'm not keeping half, but I will sell them," April said as she arranged the basket beside another basket of carrots. She paused. "You're not giving the money to Adrienne, are you?"

"No." Gisele beamed and leaned forward to whisper, "I'm saving up to run away!"

"You're–"

"Shhh!" Gisele hushed her friend. "If word gets back to Adrienne, she might lock me in the barn forever."

"Of course." April nodded, then drew in a deep breath. "It's only...wait." Her eyes narrowed, and she studied Gisele. "Why now? Why not all those times when I told you to leave before?"

"Because," Gisele said slowly, unable to stop the ridiculous smile from spreading across her face, "I think I might have found someone to help me."

April studied her for a moment longer before her eyes nearly popped. "It's a man!"

Gisele put her hands up. "April, it's not what you think–"

"Oh, no. It's definitely what I think. You're blushing already! Gisele, tell me everything!"

Unable to contain her excitement any longer, Gisele did, omitting only the parts she thought Emile might wish to keep to himself. She felt like she was Fran's age again, giggling and blushing like a mindless idiot. But Fran was fourteen, and such behavior was expected of someone her age. Of Gisele's? Not so much.

April didn't mind, though. When Gisele was done telling her story, April grabbed her by the arm and dragged Gisele behind the stall with her.

"Gisele, I'm going to say this once," April whispered fiercely. "Marry this man immediately."

"He's visited me twice for a midday meal," Gisele scoffed. "That's hardly–"

"I mean it, Gisele. Get out of this place while you have the chance!"

"But–"

"Your mother would want you to." April drew Gisele into a tight hug. "You know she would."

APRIL'S WORDS were still echoing in Gisele's head as she made her way to the outskirts of town where Adrienne had instructed her to go. But the closer she got to the far end of the last street, the less she thought about Emile, and the more she remembered her misgivings from that morning.

Adrienne had been right. Gisele *had* passed by this house all her life. But she'd never seen anyone come in or out, nor had she any idea that someone was still living there. The house was rickety and crooked, and the whole thing was a charred shade of black, as though a fire had devoured its innards but left its shell. As children, Gisele and her friends had referred to the place as the Black Gate, named for the creaky black gate that swung on its bent hinges even when there was no wind. As if sharing her trepidation, Gisele's little birds grew still and silent and sat quietly within her wreath.

Adrienne's godmother lived here?

A violent shiver rippled through Gisele's entire body, and for the briefest moment, she considered returning to the place where she cut wood and waiting for Emile. She would ask him to please hire her out to whatever rich relative of his needed a maid. Living and dying as a servant was preferable to going in *there.*

But this was ridiculous. She'd met Emile only twice. He seemed generous enough, but sharing his midday meal with her and carrying her away to find a new life were two very different kinds of generosity. It was too soon to throw herself at his mercy, and she didn't yet have enough money saved to pay for travel or food expenses. No, she would have to go into the house and face Adrienne's godmother...whoever she was.

Gisele just hoped April had been right in saying her eggs would fetch a high price. She didn't want to do this ever again.

The gate creaked louder than Gisele had ever heard it as she pushed it open to walk through. The flat stones that led up to the house were all cracked and worn smooth, crunching beneath her feet as she went. Large plants Gisele had never seen before grew wild all over the yard, and the air behind the gate seemed colder than it had on the other side. Still, Gisele forced herself on. Once across the yard, she made her way up the uneven wooden steps and raised her hand to knock.

Foolish as it was, she suddenly wished for the faerie who had gifted her the wreath.

"Hello?" she called out. "I'm Adrienne's stepdaughter. She sent me to fetch something!"

Silence.

Gisele was considering going home and telling Adrienne that no one was there when the door finally creaked open. No one was behind it.

A chill raced through Gisele's body again as she stepped slowly inside. The interior was nearly as dark as it had looked from the outside. All of the windows were boarded, and one single lamp burned from its place on the floor beside a bed. The air smelled strongly of eucalyptus and something else Gisele couldn't name.

"Hello?" she called again.

"In here." The words were nearly a hiss. As Gisele's eyes adjusted to the dark, she realized that a weak light was coming from the room beyond the one she was in. Carefully, she made her way into the second room to find an impossibly aged woman sitting at a table covered in various dried, powdery substances.

Gisele and the old woman spent a long moment looking at one another. The woman's skin looked as though it had never seen the sun. In the weak light, it appeared chalky and thin. Her eyes, however, were as dark as her skin was pale, and there was very little white visible in them. The same chill that had greeted Gisele at the gate whistled now, blowing her hair about her even though she was indoors. The dark eyes traveled up and down Gisele's person. They stopped and narrowed when they reached the top of Gisele's head.

"So," the woman hissed again, "Adrienne sent you." The corners of her thin mouth turned up slightly. "You must be Gisele."

Gisele knew it was likely that her stepmother had discussed her with this woman before. She would have had to when asking the woman to remove Simone's curse. But the casual way the woman said her name made her desire to take a step back.

"Adrienne sent me to fetch a...remedy." Gisele had to force the words out. "She said it would be ready today."

The old woman simply smiled, and the room grew colder.

"Yes, the wax," she finally said, drawing each word out like a snake. She nodded at a shelf to Gisele's left. "Take the third bottle down. That's right. The brown one. Give it to Adrienne. She'll know what to do with it."

Unable to help herself, Gisele asked, "This will make Simone well again?"

"Doubtful. I told Adrienne I would need more substance before I made it. But she insisted on trying." The old woman stretched out her neck toward Gisele, much like a turtle. "You do know that Adrienne is my goddaughter, do you not?"

Gisele nodded and blinked. As soon as she did, she felt something on her cheek and let out a shriek when she realized the old woman was inches from her face. She lifted a gnarled hand and ran it through Gisele's loose hair. "Good," she hissed, staring at the hair as it slipped through her fingers. "And if you're ever in the mood to be insolent, just remember that." Her eyes settled once again on the wreath, and though her hand remained at the level of Gisele's shoulder, Gisele got the distinct feeling that this woman wanted desperately to touch it.

Without thinking, Gisele turned and fled so fast she nearly tripped down the uneven steps. Only when she was out in the sunlight with the wind blowing the smell of fresh soil and lavender around her did she realize the other smell that she'd failed to recognize in the house.

It was the smell of death.

A HALF-HOUR PASSED before Gisele felt calm enough to return to April's market stall. She didn't want to scare April or her family, but the feeling of urgency that had hummed slightly beneath her consciousness before now roared like a bear.

She needed to escape Adrienne and all the darkness that followed in her wake. And the only person Gisele believed capable of helping her escape was Emile. But that brought her back to the trouble of their very brief acquaintance. She wanted to trust him. She yearned for it. But ever-present in the back of her mind were stories of wayward faerie youth who enjoyed luring young, gullible women away from their families, gaining their trust and even their love, only to turn on them in the most heinous ways in the end. And yet, after what she had just witnessed...

A month. She would give Emile a month. If he continued to visit her for one more month, remaining a gentleman all the while, she would ask him for help in the end. In the meantime, she would do her best to stay out of Adrienne's way. She would curb her sharp tongue and become invisible to the best of her abilities. Hopefully, the bottle in her basket would break the faerie's curse on Simone, leaving Adrienne one less reason to hate her.

But as she collected her money and gave her friend a hug, Gisele swore to herself that anyone could endure anything for one month. No matter how it happened, by the time the moon rose full again, somehow, Gisele would be free.

NINE

Gisele was convinced that the chilling cold of the old woman's cottage would follow her forever. The moment the sun went down each night, the memory of the woman's fingers in her hair haunted her, and her skin prickled as though the knobby fingers were still hovering just over her skin.

With each day spent in the sun, however, and each time Emile came to visit, the more Gisele began to feel like her old self.

At least, that's what she tried to tell herself.

Two and a half weeks after the terrifying trip to the village, her promise to herself weighed heavier than ever on her mind. Emile had come that day, as he had continued to come every few days, and was currently regaling her with stories of his boyhood mischief as they ate. She should have enjoyed his stories, and she was trying. But she hadn't been able to escape to the village to sell more eggs, and the awareness that she had only one week kept her mind from focusing on her stories as she should.

"I was convinced I'd gotten away with it." Emile shrugged. "Little did I know that our cook can apparently see everything, even when she's not in the room."

Gisele made herself smile as she knew she ought to. "What did she do?"

"Well," he said, leaning his head back thoughtfully, "she grabbed me by the scruff of the neck and dragged me outside, where she proceeded to hang me upside-down over the garden by my feet."

Despite her inner musings, Gisele chuckled. "What did your father say?"

Emile gave her a dry grin. "I deserved it. I knew it. He knew it. Everyone knew it. So he let me get my just reward, and I never stole tarts from the kitchen again." His smile disappeared, and he tilted his head. "Gisele, what's wrong?"

"What? Oh, I'm just...thinking."

"You've been thinking a lot these past few weeks," he said softly. "Do you want to tell me what it is you're thinking about?"

Gisele studied him for a long moment. His hair was still slightly damp from the sweat that had dripped down his temples as they worked, and he'd shed his fine coat when he'd arrived, revealing a much thinner, more practical shirt beneath.

All to help her cut wood.

This man, for all his riches and whatever title he held—for she was sure he held one—had come faithfully every two or three days to help her cut wood. And each time he came, he'd bring more than enough food as well. Enough, even, to ensure she had some left for the rest of that day and the next. He'd asked nothing of her in return for doing all of this, and he'd been every bit the gentleman, never seeking to seduce or even touch her.

And even if he'd done only half of that, he still would have done far more for her than her father had in a long time.

If there was a man Gisele wanted to trust, it was Emile. And yet...

"Who are you?" she asked before her courage fled her.

Emile's eyes widened. "In...what way?" he asked. He must have seen her disappointment, however, because he hurried to add, "I mean, are you referring to my father's line or my title or something else? I only want to know so I can better answer your question."

Gisele took another deep breath. "I want to trust you." She rubbed her thumbs over the waxy skin of the apple in her hands. "You obviously have some interest in me, or you wouldn't keep returning to help me do manual labor and then eat lunch with the daughter of a woodcutter. And you're obviously well-to-do." She gestured to the coat he'd tossed onto the rock. "You also wield power and influence to some degree. But I need to know..." She let her words die, praying she hadn't offended him. Praying he would understand.

"That's...only fair," he said with a wary smile. The smile, however, didn't touch his eyes. Instead, they looked...afraid?

"I often keep my parentage quiet. Not as a trick, but because people who learn of it often find they want more."

Gisele willed her eyes to meet his. "Do you believe that of me?"

He stared back. "I don't. However," he cringed slightly, "it might change the way you see me. And I'm not sure I—"

"Gisele!"

Gisele and Emile whipped their heads around to see Gisele's father striding down the hill toward the clearing. His expression was dark. "Who's this?"

Gisele wanted to scream. After abandoning her for weeks with no hint as to when he would return, her father finally decided to come back just when she was finally going to learn what she needed to know most.

"Good morning, sir," Emile said, standing and going to shake hands with her father. "You must be Gisele's father."

"Aye," said her father, looking Emile up and down, bristling like a cat. Gisele guessed he had a number of curt words he wanted to say, but her father wasn't stupid. Gisele saw him glance at Emile's steed and then the fine coat on the rock. This young man, whoever he was, could probably have her father's land if he so desired it with the snap of his fingers. Her father was a well-respected man in the community, but he was still just a woodcutter. With seemingly great difficulty, her father cleared his throat.

"It's...very kind of you to condescend to sup with my daughter," he said, sounding very much as though it was the opposite of kind. "We're far from the world out here. She doesn't get many visitors."

She doesn't get any, Gisele wanted to say. But she mashed her lips shut.

"Your daughter's company is as pleasing as she is lovely," Emile said with a slight bow and a wink at Gisele. Gisele stupidly grinned.

"He's been helping me cut wood, Father," she said. "Wasn't that kind?" *He was doing your work,* she added in her thoughts.

"How much...um, should I pay you for your labor?" her father asked stiffly.

"I've been paid more than enough by the time spent in her company," Emile said. As he spoke the sweet words, however, something in his eyes changed, and his easy smile became hard. "It's a pity she has to work so much with no time to rest. And a shame her stepmother keeps forgetting to send her food."

Gisele's father's brows rose slightly, and Gisele knew he comprehended what Emile had *not* said.

"Um, yes," he mumbled, not looking at Gisele. "Food has been somewhat rationed this spring. What with the blight and the chickens and all."

Gisele didn't realize she had been hoping until that moment. Hoping that her father would come to his senses and see what a vile serpent he had brought into their home. She had hoped that, if anything, his time away would make him miss her and think of her the way he had when she was small.

Or if that was too much, he could have at least had the decency to look mortified.

But he didn't. He didn't even look that surprised.

"I'm afraid I do need to go," Emile said, turning to Gisele. Then, to her surprise, he gently took her face in his hand. His touch was like fire, the kind she knew immediately could chase away the old woman's chill forever. She suddenly hoped he wouldn't let go.

In an even softer voice, he added. "Will you be all right?"

In that moment, Gisele realized that for all she didn't know about Emile, she trusted him more than her own father.

Secretly, she now realized, even unbeknownst to herself, she'd been harboring hopes that when her father came back, and he learned all that had happened since his departure, he would regain his senses and sweep her up in his arms protectively as he had done when she was a little girl.

But he hadn't done that. Instead, he had made excuses. Again.

Gisele knew she ought to beg Emile to take her with him. There was nothing in her home that she needed. Adrienne had claimed her mother's few pieces of jewelry. Emile, Gisele knew in her heart, would make sure that she had everything she needed and more. She knew from the way his green eyes were searching hers now that he would take her the moment she asked. All she had to do was give the word.

But Gisele wasn't ready to go. Not yet. She still had words for her father. Words that would best be spoken unheard by the rest of the world. So she nodded but took hold of Emile's other hand, amazed at her own daring, but not willing to let it go.

"Come back soon, though?" Her voice wavered slightly. "We're not done with our conversation." She did the best she could to give him a smile.

Gently, he turned her face and bent, brushing the lightest, softest of kisses across her cheek.

"Anything," he whispered.

Gisele's stomach did joyful flips.

Then Emile straightened, and the gentle smile on his face was replaced with a hard one which he aimed at her father. "Sir, I'm sure we'll meet again." Not waiting for her father to answer, Emile turned and walked back to his horse. Gisele mourned the loss of his hands, even as he tucked away his axe. With one last look at her, a look of intensity that Gisele had never seen the like of on his face, he rode off into the trees.

"And who," her father thundered as soon as he was gone, "was that?"

"His name is Emile." Gisele folded her arms and turned to face her father.

"And just how did you and this Emile meet?"

"He got lost a few weeks ago. I helped him find his way to the right road. But before he left, he noticed I had nothing to eat, so he shared his lunch."

"And he's been visiting ever since, I gather?" Her father folded his arms as well.

"Yes." Gisele sniffed. "He has."

"Gisele," her father scoffed. "I thought you were smarter than that! Letting strange men court you with no chaperone. No one else to see! What if he took it into his head to–"

Gisele saw red.

"How dare you?" she exploded.

Her father froze. "*Excuse* me?"

"How *dare* you waltz back into my life after leaving me for *weeks* with that viper you call your *wife*, and pretend that you care about my well-being?" Gisele glared up at her father, the words that had been building inside of her spilling out like a river overflowing with snow melt. "You were gone for nearly three weeks! *Three. Weeks!*"

"I had to sell—"

"When Mother was alive, you were gone for four days at the most!" Gisele's breath was coming faster now. "And you didn't even take that much wood! What in all the realms could you have been doing for two and a half weeks?"

"You'll hold your tongue, Gisele!" her father growled. His chest swelled, and he seemed to grow several inches in height as he fumed. But Gisele was past the point of caring.

"No, I will *not* hold my tongue! Because if you had bothered to come back when you should have, you could have seen the bruises Adrienne—the woman I warned you not to marry—left on my legs the day you left!" Angry tears welled, but Gisele didn't even bother trying to stop them. "She's been so incensed with me that she's barely fed me enough to keep me alive! If it hadn't been for Emile, I would have had to forage for my food like an animal! And did you know her godmother is a witch? Oh, yes. She lives in the Black Gate house at the edge of town. She made me go there two weeks ago to get what she hoped was a cure for Simone's curse! But instead of curing her, it only made her hiccup crickets for a day instead!"

Gisele marched toward her father until she had to tilt her head up to glare at him. "I have been beaten, starved, and treated like a slave. And you *know* that if Mother could see this, she would be rolling in her grave!"

To Gisele's satisfaction, his eyes had grown wide at the mention of her bruises, and they had continued to look more shocked with each revelation. Finally, when she was done shouting, he was silent.

As she waited, Gisele realized she was holding her breath.

Would he break? Was it possible for the veneer he'd created to fall away? For as much as she wanted freedom, Gisele realized that what she wanted–more than anything–was to have her father back. To find the man who had once sung her to sleep and whispered prayers in her ear at night, who had held her tightly in his strong arms when the wolves howled outside, and kissed her head softly just as she drifted into dreams.

And for a moment, she thought she might have him.

But then he sighed, and his eyes dropped to the ground. Without a word, he loaded a bundle of wood pieces onto his back and began to trudge back toward the house.

"Don't forget the axe," he called over his shoulder.

And then, he was gone.

For once, Gisele's birds were silent.

Gisele stood frozen until he was out of sight. Then she picked up her axe and threw it before letting out the scream she'd been holding inside. But once the scream was gone, the anger inside her seemed to dissipate as well. And the only thing she could do was fall on the large rock and let herself sob.

TEN

Gisele's father set out again the next day before dawn. Gisele didn't see him go, nor did he step in to whisper that he was leaving as he once would have. She only knew because she'd awakened early to the sound of footsteps in the hall. She lay in bed listening as he wished Adrienne a good morning in a low voice, promising to return in two weeks' time. Then he paused and closed the door.

Again.

In the old days, before her mother had fallen sick, he would have taken Gisele with him. They wouldn't have been gone long, maybe five days at most before they returned. Since marrying Adrienne, however, he seemed to leave more and more. And he never took Gisele.

Gisele was up and changing clothes half a minute later. She wasn't about to wait for Adrienne to find her this time. The moment she was decent, she grabbed a basket and hurried out to the chicken coop. She would get her eggs then take them out to the clearing with her. Then, if he came today, perhaps Emile would have the time to take her into the village to sell her eggs. It would be much faster if he let her ride on his horse with him. Her heart thumped unevenly at the thought.

But more important than sitting that close to him, she reminded herself, would be the money those eggs could help her bring in. Then she could plead with Emile to help her find a post, perhaps at the home of one of his friends or relatives.

Whether he could take her or not, she knew that once she saw Emile long enough to tell him her plans, she would never be coming home.

Or, her wayward heart whispered, perhaps he wouldn't want her to run away to a servant's post. Maybe...just maybe, he would want to keep her, too.

"I'm being foolish," she told her little birds as she gathered the hens' eggs. "He has a title and power and responsibility. Even if he did feel something for me, he wouldn't–and probably couldn't–stoop that low. And...don't get finicky with me. You know I'm telling the truth." The little birds had begun twittering angrily at her as she spoke. "Even if," she continued firmly, "he did want more, there's no way his family would allow it."

As she gathered the eggs and bathed in the dewy air of the morning, Gisele began to relax. She always relaxed outside, though. It was one of the reasons she didn't mind cutting wood with her father. The feel of the soft earth beneath her boots and the clean air always made her heaviest problems seem a little lighter than they had been in the dark of night.

Unfortunately, the soft soil muffled the sounds of Adrienne's footsteps behind Gisele, and she didn't hear her stepmother's approach.

"You little vixen!" A strong hand grabbed Gisele by the arm and yanked her around. Adrienne glowered down at her with a ferocity Gisele hadn't seen before. "You viper!" she hissed before raising her hand and striking Gisele across the face.

Gisele dropped her eggs, but she didn't dare look down. Instead, she stumbled back several steps and covered her stinging cheek and nose with her hands, but Adrienne only followed, her head and shoulders lowered like a wolf stalking its prey. Gisele felt something wet on her lips and glanced down to find blood dripping from her nose.

"Secretly carousing with rich young men while your sister wastes away at home!" Adrienne continued. "I never liked you, it's true. But I never thought I'd be sheltering a loose harpy beneath my roof!"

Gisele glanced around her. The chicken yard was connected to the barn by a back door, which Adrienne, who was far taller than Gisele, was blocking. The fence was only waist high, but it was still too tall for Gisele to jump in her dress. She was trapped.

"Be grateful you have that wreath!" Adrienne continued to stalk forward. "Because I would do far worse to you now if it didn't mean involving some nosy faerie!"

A faerie Gisele very much wished would appear at any minute. But none came, even though Gisele's birds were chirping out cries of alarm. Gisele's back hit the fence. She had no place left to run.

"Listen to me now." Adrienne grabbed Gisele by the shoulder and yanked her so hard, Gisele cried out in pain. She tried to escape from her stepmother's grasp, but just as Adrienne was too beautiful, she was also too strong. "Because I will not make this threat twice!"

Gisele reached back and grasped the fence behind her, wishing her father hadn't built it to be so sturdy. If only she could push it over!

"If you don't give up this foolishness," Adrienne hissed, sending spit all over Gisele's face, "you'll regret it. Faerie or no faerie, I'll make sure my godmother finds a fitting charm for you. No matter what the cost."

"Why are you doing this?" Gisele asked, her voice trembling slightly. "I've done nothing to you! Why can't you just let me be?"

Adrienne studied her keenly for a moment before letting go of Gisele's shoulder. She went over to where Gisele had dropped her basket of eggs and picked it up before returning to face Gisele.

"I was the daughter of an earl," she said in a strange voice. "I always expected to marry nobility, or even royalty. But then I met my first husband. And I fell in love."

Gisele pressed her back against the fence again, but it didn't budge.

"My parents tried to talk me out of it," Adrienne continued, holding a cracked egg up to examine it. "My father swore to disown me. My mother sobbed her heart out. But I gave everything up for the poverty-stricken mason who had stolen my heart." She looked up at the sky and frowned, her eyes unfocused. "But once I realized what it meant to give everything up, it was too late to go back. And I went from being the most sought-after woman in this part of the country to washing my own filth off in the river and my clothes with me. And when I gave birth to my baby girl, I swore that somehow, I would find a way to make sure she never had to live the nightmarish existence I was then eking out."

She looked down and focused on Gisele again. "You told your father that you found it suspicious the way my first husband died. Yes, don't look so surprised. He told me about that, too. And do you know what?" A smile began to spread across Adrienne's face until her eyes were narrowed to near slits. "You were right."

A chill raced up Gisele's spine. She had indeed found it strange that Adrienne's husband would die just after Gisele's mother had. Supposedly, he had fallen and hit his head on a brick. But several townspeople who had been there to witness the accident had claimed that there was no reason he should have fallen. He hadn't even tripped.

Another shudder passed through Gisele. She didn't know how, but she knew that Adrienne had somehow killed her husband.

Adrienne was no longer smiling. She appeared to be trembling as well. "I'll freely admit to you that I offered my husband in exchange for my daughter's unrivaled beauty. And while I know you'll judge me for it, I had no other *choice*! That kind of magic doesn't come without a cost! It can't be performed without a sacrifice of some sort!"

Tears began streaming down Adrienne's face, but she continued to speak. "I went to my godmother, desperate to raise Simone from the pit I'd sunk into. And when she told me the price, I was willing to pay it! I would do anything to keep my baby girl from living in the filth and muck she had been born in! So when she told me a life would be needed to pay for such power, I offered up my husband. She took his life and remade it into a gift that no other woman could rival." She gave Gisele a wry smile. "There was even some left over for me."

Gisele stared at her stepmother, wishing more than ever that she could be sure she would outrun Adrienne to the barn door. Adrienne's story had brought back the all-too potent memory of the stench of death in the Black Gate cottage, and Gisele suddenly wanted to vomit.

"You can judge me all you want!" Adrienne continued, her words barely audible as she began to sob. "But I'm not going to sit by and allow my daughter to suffer poverty and helplessness as I did after I married. She *will* marry well, and when your father is no longer useful to me, I'll be finished with him too."

"Why are you telling me all of this?" Gisele whispered, too horrified to do anything but stare. What game was Adrienne playing at?

Adrienne took another step toward her until she was towering over Gisele. "Who will you tell? Your father won't believe you. He doesn't want to." She smirked and shrugged. Then she leaned over Gisele once again. "And," she whispered, inches from Gisele's face, "I also want you to know just how far I'm willing to go to get my daughter where she deserves to be." She straightened and examined the eggs in Gisele's basket once more.

Gisele knew she should try to run. But Adrienne still had her pinned in the corner of the yard.

"Oops," Adrienne said, still studying the basket. "You missed a few." She met Gisele's gaze, then dropped the basket once more. It hit the ground with an audible crack, and when Gisele dared to glance down, every single egg inside oozed yellow.

Adrienne smiled slightly before turning and heading back to the barn door. But before she went inside, she turned once more.

"I don't care a fig for what happens to you and your father once I've gotten what I came for. His standing in the community is decent enough for my purposes, but I never intended to be a woodcutter's wife for long." Her eyes narrowed. "You should know, however, that you will suffer more than you can imagine if you get in my way. I've sacrificed too much to lose it all now." Then she smiled again.

This smile, however, wasn't the cynical, mocking grin Gisele was used to. For one horrifying moment, Adrienne's beautiful human features twisted into something indescribably inhuman. Her pupils narrowed to vertical slits, and her skin melted into something mottled and greenish-gray.

But then the Adrienne Gisele knew was back again,

stunningly beautiful as ever. And yet...Gisele stayed rooted to the spot.

"As you can see," Adrienne said, "I'm willing to give what I must to get what I want." She smiled slightly again. "Oh, and don't go down to the clearing today. Simone will go for you."

And with that, she was gone.

CHAPTER
ELEVEN

Gisele remained near the house after that, vacillating between running away immediately and hoping for the best, or delaying until she could gather and escape with what she needed and being better prepared to travel. Unfortunately, her money was hidden in her room. If no one saw her, she could make it in and out in under a minute. But she had no doubt Adrienne was waiting for her to do just that. Her little show with Gisele's eggs this morning had made it clear that she knew what Gisele was up to. Getting her money unseen was impossible. And yet, without it, Gisele wouldn't stand a chance of survival on the road.

She could always go to April's home, she mused as she broke the soil in the garden. April's family would welcome Gisele with open arms. But Adrienne had friends in the community, and not many days would pass before someone told Adrienne where Gisele had gone. And Gisele would rather die than involve her friend's family in Adrienne's dark games.

She could run to the clearing and try to find Emile before he looked for her. But several times, she'd seen Adrienne peek out the window at her and smile slightly before letting the curtain fall again. If she left, Adrienne would guess where she had gone, and Gisele had no doubt that her step-mother would use any means to stop her...including means that had come from the Black Gate cottage witch.

But what would happen if Gisele did stay? What if Simone's mother had given her sort of charm that might entrap Emile against his will? It wasn't likely. Simone had used natural means to attract her previous suitor. But now that Adrienne knew that there was a man of title coming often to the clearing, Gisele wondered what else Adrienne would sacrifice to make him Simone's?

And, of course, beneath all her worry, Gisele felt a deep sense of shame. Shame at not fighting harder. Shame at being too weak to stand up to her stepmother. Darkness had been threatening to swallow her once happy home. And she had done very little to stop it.

What if she had tried to stop it? Would she have won if she'd fought back? Most likely not. Adrienne was taller and stronger than Gisele, which was odd, as she never did any of the heavy household chores. But still...Gisele should have tried.

Well, she would try now. Gisele stood and wiped the sweat off her brow. The next time Adrienne looked at her, she would wait until the curtain had fallen again, and as soon as Adrienne was satisfied, Gisele would race down to the field and hide in the trees from which Emile always emerged. And she would stay there until he came again, even if it meant sleeping in the woods. He didn't deserve to fall prey to Adrienne's wiles.

"Gisele?"

Gisele's head snapped up at the sound of Emile's voice. Relief so potent she nearly burst into tears washed through her. But just behind that relief was the now-familiar shame. She quickly looked down again as he dismounted and strode over to her. The bruise blossoming on her cheek would be a dead giveaway of her cowardice, and a witness to her weakness.

But then a new kind of fear, one stronger than her other fears, struck her. What if Adrienne looked outside now?

"Gisele, why weren't you in the clearing?" he asked, coming to stand in front of her. Gisele kept her head down as she worked the hoe into the soil.

"You need to leave," she said in a low voice. "My step-mother might come out any minute."

"Not until you talk to me." She could hear the frown in his voice.

"Emile, you need to go. I'll meet you–"

"Gisele." His voice hardened in a way she hadn't heard it before. "What happened?"

"I'm telling you, you need to–"

He didn't let her finish. Gently but firmly, he took her chin and lifted her face so she had to look at him. And she knew the moment he saw. His eyes became like flint, and his jaw audibly clicked.

"Did your father do this?" he asked in a low, dangerous voice.

She shook her head and tried to look back down, but he gently lifted her face again.

"Then who–"

"My stepmother." She glanced back at the house again. Had the curtain fluttered? Or was that her imagination?

"Why?"

"My father told her about you, it seems." Gisele's voice was suddenly bitter as the memory of her argument with her father came back to her. "She's angry that I wouldn't give you to my stepsister."

His mouth fell slightly open. "You mean...that awful girl who yelled at me when I asked where you were?"

"The inhumanly beautiful one?" Gisele asked, bracing herself for when he said yes.

"The one who yelled, 'Dirty creatures,' over and over again," He shuddered slightly. For some reason, this made Gisele feel better than she had all morning.

"That...would be her," Gisele said, almost tempted to smile.

Emile let go of her and began to pace back and forth, muttering slightly to himself as he did.

"You really do need to go," Gisele said, glancing back at the house once more. "My stepmother is–"

But Emile stopped pacing and took Gisele's hands in his. They were rough and warm, and Gisele found herself stupidly wishing he wouldn't let go. She needed something to hold onto, and now, despite her words, she clung to him for dear life.

"You can't stay here," he said in a low, urgent voice. "But I know what you should do."

"I know." Gisele nodded. "I have a little money saved. And...and I was hoping that perhaps...perhaps you could help find me a position somewhere. A scullery maid or a servant or–"

"A scullery maid?" He made a face. "No, Gisele. You're not understanding. What you need to do is marry me."

It was Gisele's turn to stare. "I...what?"

"I can protect you," he leaned closer, and Gisele was washed in whatever sweet, musky scent he wore. "You can be happy and safe, and they can never hurt you again." His green eyes were brighter and more intense than she'd ever seen them, and she wondered if he was aware that he was rubbing his thumbs gently over her knuckles.

Gisele stuttered, at a loss for words. "But my step-mother–She's...she has powerful connections. You can't know what she's capable of. That's why I haven't run away yet." She shook her head slightly. "You might want to protect me, but the darkness she could bring upon you and everyone in your household would be...unthinkable." She paused, then looked up at him again. "Also...why would you want to marry me?"

For the first time that day, a ghost of his impish grin returned. "I've always thought you were charming and beautiful and intelligent. But when I heard what Mother Dove did for you, I knew that you were good most of all."

"Good?" Gisele echoed.

He nodded eagerly. "Mother Dove! The one who gifted you that wreath."

Gisele gaped. "How do you know who gave me the wreath? It was a faerie. I'm sure of it."

But Emile shook his head. "Mother Dove is a faerie-*blessed* dove, gifted with languages–animal and human–and a small amount of her own magic. She was set to watch over the birds in this country. Also," he grinned, "she told me."

"Then...how do you know her?" Gisele asked.

He reddened slightly. "When I was young, I was climbing trees. I spotted a nest with beautiful blue eggs, and I was in the process of taking one to bring back to my mother when something sharp and fast attacked me from above."

Gisele frowned. "Was it her?" Was this story supposed to endear the bird to her?

"It was. She scolded me into returning the egg to the nest and forbade me from ever stealing eggs from nests again." His small smile grew. "I was terrified to go outside for weeks. Because every time I did, she found me and began scolding me and telling me what a good boy I ought to be."

"She doesn't sound very pleasant," Gisele said.

"I didn't think so at first. But eventually, I realized that she had stopped scolding me for stealing eggs long ago, and had been giving me wise advice instead. Now she's one of my most trusted advisers." He took Gisele's right hand in both of his and pressed her palm softly against his lips. Gisele nearly melted at the tenderness of his touch.

"So when I saw your gift and heard your story, I knew immediately who had been at work. And that you would merit so high in Mother Dove's estimation as to become a companion to her children, I knew immediately why she had purposefully gotten me so lost the day we met." He softly traced Gisele's unbruised cheek. "She wanted me to meet you. And for a woman to have Mother Dove's trust is the highest praise I could ever wish for in a wife."

Now that he explained it...it all made sense. As did Gisele's strange dreams about the motherly voice and the little birds. But Gisele wasn't ready just yet. She wanted to be. And yet, if he jumped in now but then changed his mind...

It just might kill her.

"But marriage." She shook her head. "That's...for the rest of our lives. And you barely know me. Besides, as I told you. My stepmother is an evil woman. And she has a source of dark magic at her disposal." Gisele shivered. "I don't doubt your intentions. But if you marry me, I have no doubt that she'll take revenge on you and your house for doing so."

Emile drew her into his arms, and while Gisele knew she ought to push him away, she took a deep breath and soaked in his solid embrace. If she wasn't careful, it would be very easy to feel safe, even if she knew she wasn't.

"If any man has the means to protect you," he said into her hair, "it's me."

Gisele opened her eyes. Then she leaned back to study him. "What do you mean by that?" She knew he was at least a lord's son. Maybe even a duke, but what could a duke do against a witch?

"Are you the son of an earl?" she asked.

He gave her a sheepish smile. "I'm not."

"A duke?"

Again, he smiled and shook his head.

She frowned. "Then what—"

"My name...is Emile," he said slowly, "but that is not my first name."

Gisele stared at him.

"My full name," he continued, "is Julien...Emile...Antione...Andre Yannick. Son of King Antione III."

Gisele clapped a hand over her mouth. "You mean you're..." She couldn't utter the words.

He nodded slowly. "Crown prince of Reinier."

"You're...you're the crown prince? *Crown* prince?"

"Shhh!" He put his finger to his lips and quickly looked around. She did, too, but for the moment, they still seemed safe.

"Why didn't you tell me?" she hissed, her head reeling. A small part of her brain reminded her that she ought not to be yelling at the crown prince. She should instead be kneeling. So as her mind continued to spin, she automatically began to drop to one knee. Before she could reach the ground, however, he pulled her gently back up.

"And that," he said with a touch of disgust, "is why I kept my identity a secret."

"But–"

"Because I *like* you. And I wanted to get to know you. But no one gets to *know* the prince. As soon as they find out who I am, they grovel or cower or try to find a way to get something out of me."

Despite Gisele's current state of confusion, indignation rose inside her. "And you thought I would try to get something out of you? Your wish, perhaps?"

"No!" he said quickly. "I was going to tell you yesterday, but your father interrupted."

That was true. Her father had interrupted. But it didn't help soften the blow. Gisele shook her head and squeezed her eyes shut before opening them again. "Surely...surely your father wants you to marry a princess or a duchess or someone like that."

Emile–Julien shrugged. "He does." Then his eyes glittered. "However, I am known throughout the palace for generally doing as I please."

As unwise as it seemed–for her mother had raised her to be wary and shrewd–Gisele was suddenly aware that she wanted nothing more than to leap into his arms and beg him to take her. A handsome prince had just appeared before her and asked her to marry him, promising to protect and keep her for the rest of their lives. Even if he wasn't madly in love with her, he was gentle and kind. After her mother's death and her father's abandonment, Gisele would take those qualities over passion any day. And yet...

"You really want me?" she asked in a small voice, a vision of Simone's incomparable beauty flashing before her eyes. "More than someone like Simone?"

He put his hands on Gisele's waist and drew her toward him. A bold move, but one she wasn't about to shake off. His hands were like anchors, and right now, she desperately needed something to ground her.

"What I want is a woman of excellent character who will make a good queen over my people one day. I want someone who will rule my kingdom with justice and strength. And you," he tapped her nose, "are such a woman." His eyes sparkled again. "Although, I will admit that I also think you're quite beautiful, and I've wanted to kiss you for a long time."

"But..." She swallowed, trying to wake herself up from the dream she knew couldn't be real. "We hardly know each other."

"Then why not," he said, lifting her hand to his mouth once more, "spend the rest of our lives becoming the closest of friends?"

Gisele wanted to. She wanted it–him so much. And yet...

She glanced back at the cottage once more and tried to think fast. She had prayed for a way out. And now it was standing in front of her, holding her hands and wearing an incredibly charming smile. She could leave this place behind and never be treated like a servant again. No more pain and insults. Always to be treasured and loved.

A chance to start again.

Then a horrible realization dawned on her.

"My stepmother..." She shook her head slowly. "Her godmother is a witch."

"You said that."

"No, you don't understand." Gisele glared at the cottage. "Once she finds out that I've married you–the ultimate prize–she's going to do terrible things. It would endanger you and the kingdom. I can't have that on my conscience."

"And might I remind you that my father is king. He has lines of communication with the faeries, and as witchcraft is strictly forbidden by the law, they can help him track this witch down and deal with her justly, as well as arresting your stepmother and making sure she never sees the light of day again."

"On what grounds would you arrest her?" Gisele asked. "She's not a witch."

"No." He brushed his finger across her bruised cheek. "But beating the prince's betrothed is a rather serious crime."

"I wasn't your betrothed when it happened."

"My intended, then." He gave her another mischievous grin. "Because I've been intending to marry you for the last two weeks." He dropped to one knee, cupping her hands in his. "Please, Gisele. Don't make me use my wish."

Gisele gave a very unladylike snort. "You can't wish for anyone to fall in love with you."

"I don't think falling in love is the problem," he gave her a soft, knowing smile.

Gisele hesitated a moment more. Could she do this in good conscience? But then she remembered how Mother Dove had arranged everything so well, and she recalled April's words that Gisele should escape any way she could. Also, the prince was right. Because Gisele wanted to be his beloved more than she had ever wanted anything in her life.

Gisele's mother had left her. Her father had abandoned her. But for some reason, the crown prince had not.

Unable to keep from smiling, Gisele leaned down and pressed her lips against his. And as she did, she whispered, "Yes."

TWELVE

Julien released Gisele from the kiss far too soon for her taste. But then he stood and drew her back in for another. His hands were firm but gentle as he held her close, and his lips were careful yet eager. She breathed deeply of his scent until her head spun, and all of her good sense with it. All too soon, however, he pulled away again, that hard, determined look on his face once more.

"Is there anything inside that you need? Anything you must take with you?"

Gisele almost told him she needed another kiss, but once her lips were her own again, the gravity of their situation returned.

She nearly responded that she should like some of her mother's wedding china. When her parents had gotten married, they'd received a beautiful porcelain heirloom tea set that was white with little pink rosebuds on it. But no. Going back inside would give them away. And while they'd escaped notice thus far, Gisele had no idea how long they would remain unseen. Her mother would have wanted her to have the tea set, but she was also a woman of sense. More than anything, she would have wanted Gisele to escape.

"Should I leave a note for my father?" Gisele wondered slowly. "Not telling him where I went, but that I'm not coming home?"

Julien clenched his jaw. "That man doesn't deserve a second thought from you. Let him search and panic. A load of guilt would do him good. Besides, you'd have to go inside to get parchment for a note."

Gisele nodded. He was right, and the longer they delayed, the more likely they were to be seen.

"You're right. I have nothing to write with." She swallowed, suddenly feeling rather breathless. "I'll send him a message once we're...married." She blushed as she said the word. "Let's go."

Julien grinned and pecked her on the cheek once more. "Words I've wanted to hear for weeks." He led her back to his horse and knelt with his fingers clasped together, resting on his knee. The rush of doing the forbidden made Gisele's heart pound in her ears, but she put her foot on his hands and allowed him to boost her into the saddle. A moment later, he was seated behind her.

She should have been frightened as his horse carried them forward. After all, she was going to live in a place she'd never been, surrounded by people she didn't know, and had just agreed to marry a man she'd known for only three weeks. But a snow-white dove flew alongside them, singing a jubilant song, and the forests around them seemed to come alive with countless harmonies being chirped from every tree that lined the road. And with the safety of his warm chest at her back and the bright blue sky before her, Gisele smiled as she left everything she knew behind.

THE COUNTRYSIDE PASSED FAR FASTER than Gisele expected, and about two hours later, they arrived at the capital city.

"Oh," Gisele breathed as they paused at the top of a hill and looked down upon the countless rooftops, a glittering castle towering at the center of it all.

"Welcome home," Julien said, his breath warm on her ear, and his deep voice making his chest rumble pleasantly in his chest.

Gisele couldn't help smiling.

Home.

Her house hadn't felt like home in a very long time.

Her confidence began to waver, however, as they drew nearer to the castle. Cries of delight came from the people they passed on the streets as they recognized their prince, and Gisele recognized immediately that the citizens of the capital city adored him. She glanced over her shoulder at the man whom she had only known as a friend and companion until today, the man who had shared his meals and helped her chop wood. This same man wasn't the spoiled son of some earl using her to pass the time as she'd first believed. This was the heir to the throne. He had the power to grant life or death, to exercise justice and mercy, and the lives and safety of his citizens were and would always be a burden he would have to bear until the day he died.

Could she do that? Could the poor daughter of a wood-cutter be the kind of queen he needed? She hadn't even been able to stand up to her stepmother. How could she help rule a kingdom?

"I usually take the backstreets in order to avoid this kind of attention," Julien whispered in her ear.

"Why aren't we doing that now?" she whispered back.

"Because," he said, a smile in his voice, "I think the people deserve to see their future queen."

Queen.

Gisele's stomach gave a lurch.

As if to make her discomfort worse, the closer they got to the palace, the larger the cottages grew until they turned into sprawling houses and then mansions. She also became painfully aware of her dirty and slightly faded dress and the dirt that had crusted her boots and was probably on the hem of her dress. Those watching from below whispered and stared even as they waved, and Gisele felt slightly sick.

But, she reminded herself, at least she still had her wreath. In fact, her little birds seemed happier than ever. They were singing more loudly than Gisele had ever heard them.

At least someone was at ease.

By the time the palace gates opened and the prince was announced, Gisele wished she could become invisible. But it was too late to worry about that, so she simply tried to shrink back into Julien's arms as far as possible.

"Good afternoon, Sire." A short man in a cloak and fine

gray clothes came out to greet them as they came to a stop in front of a large set of doors. He bowed low as Julien handed the reins down to one of the manservants standing nearby.

"Hello, Samuel." Julien swung down from the horse, then held his hands out to help Gisele. "I'd like you to meet Gisele."

If Samuel was surprised that Julien had brought back a bedraggled woman wearing a floral wreath filled with birds, he didn't show it. He simply bowed to Gisele as well.

"Where are my parents?" Julien asked.

"They're in the throne room," Samuel answered, gesturing to another servant, who brought them both goblets of cool, clear water.

"Perfect." Julien beamed and took Gisele's hand. Gisele quickly gulped down several mouthfuls of water before managing to hand the goblet back as Julien began to drag her up the large stone steps to the palace's main door.

Everywhere they went, people bowed and curtsied, and Gisele was once again glad for her spotless wreath, as it meant she had at least one court-appropriate decoration in which she could meet the king and queen.

She was going to meet the king and queen.

"J–Julien?" she asked timidly as he strode confidently down another hall.

"Yes?" He glanced back with a smile.

"Do you think...I might have a moment to clean myself up? Before we meet your parents, I mean?"

His smile only widened. "I'll ensure you have every comfort you could ever desire once we're done."

"But won't they mind?" she panted slightly as they turned another corner. "I've just ridden two hours after working all morning in a garden."

He beamed back at her. "No." Then he glanced up and down her person and laughed. "Believe me. You're far from the dirtiest thing I've brought home."

"I'm glad to know that...I think."

He let go of her hand and laughed again, pausing before a set of double doors. The doors were at least two heads taller than he was, and carved into them were a set of ancient markings Gisele couldn't read. "And unlike my pocket full of toads, I doubt you're about to jump into my mother's hair."

His eyes glinted as he threw the doors open, then took her hand once more to lead her inside.

It was the largest room Gisele had ever seen. She could have easily fit her village's entire market inside, including the church's steeple. At the far end stood two tall, thin thrones on a dais. Each throne, while wooden, sparkled with what looked like gems. A tall, stocky man with a thick, graying beard sat in one, and an equally tall, slender woman with bright red hair sat in the other. Tapestries of various colors hung from the walls, all depicting battles or various magical creatures, and eight chandeliers swayed slightly from the ceiling. Men and women in fine clothing milled about the room, murmuring in low voices as the man on the throne talked to a knight standing before him.

Gisele's feet nearly stopped working the second she saw her monarchs, but Julien tugged her gently forward. Then he turned and faced the front of the room.

"I'd like a moment with my parents, please," he boomed, his voice echoing through the large stone hall.

Gisele wondered if some of these fine people would be annoyed that the prince had just requested, albeit politely, that they all leave. Instead of seeming offended, however, just as Samuel had done, they all simply bowed or curtsied and made their way out.

Julien hadn't been exaggerating when he'd said he was used to getting his way. And yet, as with Samuel, no one seemed to mind.

As soon as the room was clear, Gisele forgot to wonder at this. Because she was suddenly vividly aware that the king and queen were looking at her.

"Mother. Father," Julien said, towing her along behind him again. "I want you to meet Gisele."

The king and queen exchanged an unreadable glance, and as she curtsied, Gisele wanted to melt into the floor.

"Welcome, Gisele," the king said. He had the deepest voice Gisele had ever heard. He wore a thoughtful frown, but his tone wasn't unkind. "We're always glad to meet any friend of our son's." His eyes moved to Gisele's wreath, and his visible confusion grew more pronounced.

"Yes," said the queen with a steady smile. Her eyes were bright blue, and Gisele got the feeling that nothing escaped her notice.

"Gisele isn't merely a friend," Julien said, putting his hands on her shoulders. "She's going to be my bride."

The queen had joined the king in studying Gisele's singing wreath, but at this announcement, they both gave a start.

"Your..." The queen blinked. "Your...bride?"

"Yes." Julien beamed down at Gisele. She gave him a shaky smile in return. They really hadn't thought this through. She'd been so excited about escaping her home that all thought of what came next had...not been considered. And now all she could do was stand there hoping they didn't assume her to be the crown-chaser she surely appeared to be.

"But Princess Peony," the king stuttered. "Her father and I have been in talks for months..."

Gisele suddenly had the urge to cry. But as if sensing her hesitance, Julien gave her shoulders a gentle squeeze.

"Julien," she whispered, but the queen, seeming to have recovered her wits first, stood.

"So," she said as she descended the dais, a slight smile tugging at the corners of her lips, "is this where you've been disappearing to every day? Or rather, *who* you've been disappearing to?"

Julien shrugged. "Not every day, regrettably. I was unable to completely neglect my duties. But yes, this is the girl I've been courting every chance I get."

Gisele's heart nearly stopped. Julien had told her only that morning that he'd wanted to marry her for the last fortnight. But only now did his words really weigh heavily upon her. For the first time, the truth felt real. He truly had been courting her. His visits hadn't been spontaneous or thoughtless in nature. There had been no, as she'd assumed, casual hope. Almost from the start, he'd made strategic plans with the express purpose of wooing and wedding her.

Despite her embarrassment at her predicament, Gisele's

breath caught in her throat as she straightened, and she had the strange and sudden desire to wrap her arms around his chest and bury her face in it. But doing that in front of his parents was obviously out of the question, so she contented herself with reveling in the way his hands felt on her shoulders. Fortifying and wanted.

"Gisele," Julien continued. "is the woman I want as queen over our people."

"And would this," the queen asked gently, indicating to Gisele's chirping wreath, "have anything to do with it?" Then her smile fell, and her eyes narrowed. Gently, she reached up and touched Gisele's bruised cheek. "My dear, what happened?"

"I was gifted the wreath," Gisele said shyly, "by Mother Dove." Did they even know who Mother Dove was? Or had Mother Dove only made herself known to Julien? She should have asked before they arrived. "But my stepmother wanted her daughter to have it. And she grew angry when the wreath refused to be worn by someone else."

The queen's blue eyes turned to ice. She turned and looked back at her husband, who had stood and was making his way down to them as well.

"Her stepmother is involved with a witch," Julien told his father. "We escaped this morning when her stepmother wasn't looking, but I have no doubt she'll know soon enough where Gisele has gone."

Gisele swallowed hard. "My fear is that she'll attempt to take out her revenge on Julien–on the prince, I mean–and the kingdom." She shivered. "She was angrier than I've ever seen her, and she promised punishment if I disobeyed. And that was before I escaped."

"I'm disturbed to hear we have a witch within our borders at all," the king's face darkened into the same hardened expression Gisele had seen on Julien's face just that morning. "I thought we chased the last one out fourteen years ago."

"Nevertheless," the queen said, her voice gentle once again, "if you were gifted by Mother Dove, it seems there is very little to say about the matter but to welcome you to the family." Then she chuckled and shook her head.

Gisele didn't see what was funny, but when she looked at Julien, raising her brows in question, he only smiled as well. "Mother Dove might have saved me from myself more than once as a boy."

The king snorted. "You'd have been dead five times over by now if she hadn't continually intervened."

Gisele looked back at Julien. "That's more times than you told me," she said, which only made the queen laugh again.

"My dear," she said, still shaking her head, "if you have enough sense for Mother Dove to approve of you, then we certainly can't ask for anything more." She pulled Gisele into a warm, firm hug. "Welcome to the family, daughter."

Gisele nearly began to cry.

THIRTEEN

The queen walked in a slow circle around Gisele, ruffling her dress here and there as the servants put their final touches on her hair, face, and shoes. Gisele felt somewhat like a life-sized doll come to life. Her hair had been brushed until it was silkier and smoother than it had ever been, and then it had been curled and pinned onto her head with little flowers woven into the locks. Her wreath sat above it all, a crown in its own right. Because of the wreath's faerie origins, the queen and king had decided against giving her the traditional princess crown, which she would have donned after the wedding. But, as the king pointed out, it would be a shame—and somewhat dangerous—to try to remove the gift that had brought Gisele and Julien together in the first place.

Her dress had been fashioned after the wreath with pale green gossamer flowing over white silk beneath. Pink flowers had been fashioned out of silk and sewn onto the gossamer, so they gave the appearance of floating around her. The bodice was also refreshingly simple with more of the pale green, and small pink flowers lined her waist. Clear crystals were sewn into swirls between them, creating a sparkling filigree that caught the late morning light. Her arms had no silk, but only the pale green gossamer all the way down to her wrists, and her slippers were made of crystal-studded silk to match.

"Oh, Gisele," the queen sighed as she stepped back and studied her. "You're something out of a dream. No wonder my son fell head over heels for you."

Gisele laughed. "I can assure you I didn't look like this when he found me."

The queen clapped her hands. "Thank you for your help, ladies. You may go now." The room cleared immediately. Less than two minutes later, only Gisele and her future-mother-in-law remained.

"Are you ready?" the queen asked, coming to take Gisele's hands.

Gisele took a deep breath. Was she ready?

"I am, only..." She looked out the open doors to the flower-laden balcony outside. "I wish my mother could have been here."

The queen squeezed her hands and gave her a sad smile. "As do I, dear." She sighed but then studied Gisele again. "But something else is bothering you as well. Isn't it?"

Gisele wondered if the queen was quite so observant with everyone, or if she was still testing her son's bride. Either way, it would be best to tell the truth.

"I was just wondering if...you don't think he'll come to regret this. Do you?" She couldn't bring herself to look directly at the queen. "It's only that this is so fast, and he's only known me three weeks, and—"

"Gisele," the queen said, taking Gisele by the shoulders. "While I can't tell you why Julien does half the things he does, I can assure you that he never does them halfway."

Gisele couldn't help smiling. "I suppose that's so."

"It is so. Now, I'm going to go and see when they'll be ready for us. You're perfect, so stay here until I come back."

"Is Julien already supposed to be in the chapel?" Gisele asked.

"He'd better be," his mother answered wryly. "Or he's going to have the queen's wrath to contend with."

Once the door was shut, Gisele smoothed her skirts again for lack of something to do. But she hadn't been alone for more than a minute before a voice spoke from behind her.

"You'd think she didn't trust me."

Gisele stifled a small shriek as she whirled around to see two hands grasping at the bottom of the balcony. She hurried over to peer outside. There, in his military uniform, Julien hung from the ledge.

"Julien!" Gisele hissed. "You're supposed to be in the chapel! Not in my room!"

"I know, I know. Bride's surprise and all. But look." Julien hoisted himself up onto the edge of the balcony. He was blindfolded.

Gisele's mouth fell open. "You can't mean to tell me you climbed up the side of the palace blindfolded—"

"Of course not." He waved her off. "I climbed out onto

that little terrace down there with the garden. It's only a short distance up from there."

Gisele stared blankly at her soon-to-be husband, but her birds sent him sharp little chirps.

"I see I've rendered you speechless, and I will accept it as a compliment." He put his hand on his chest and bowed slightly. "But I'm not here for accolades." He reached into his military jacket, which was a dark blue with silver buttons and a silver rope–and pulled out a small box, which he held out to her. "This, my darling, is for you."

Gisele took the box, still not sure whether she would kiss him or tell his mother, and opened it. "Oh!" she breathed.

Inside the box, on a thin golden chain and nestled in a bed of velvet, was a small, pink glass rose. And it looked exceptionally like those on her wreath. With slightly shaking hands, Gisele removed it and held it up, where it sparkled in the light.

"It's not just any rose," Julien said. "I asked Mother Dove to help get the faeries to enchant it."

"Oh, Julien," Gisele breathed again, still beyond words. "What...what is it enchanted for?"

"I asked them," he said, this time in a more reverent voice, "to tie it to my heart. So wherever you're at, I'll feel myself drawn to you."

Gisele felt tears prick her eyes, and she looked up at him again. Even with the blindfold, he was so handsome as he leaned back against the balcony's railing, his hair slightly ruffled from his climb, and a small, triumphant smile on his lips.

"Julien, I..." Gisele swallowed hard. "Thank you."

"Put that on. My mother will be here again soon." His grin widened. "She's probably wondering where I am."

"Um, yes." Gisele shook her head. "You need to go. She was going to look for you."

He nodded and turned but then paused. "Before I go, would it be possible to get a small kiss–"

"Julien, go!" Gisele laughed.

Julien sighed dramatically, but he turned and did as she said. Gisele nearly had another heart attack as he swung a leg over the railing once more and then casually lowered himself down the other side, still blindfolded. Then he abruptly disappeared.

Gisele let out a shriek and ran over to the edge to see where he'd fallen, only to find him laughing as he picked himself up off the lower balcony.

"Next time I see you," he called up with a grin, "that kiss is mine."

THE CHAPEL WAS MADE of ancient white stones that glittered, and its soaring windows were made of pastel-colored stained glass. Gisele felt as though she were floating through a dream as the king led her down the aisle. His smile was kind and fatherly, and Gisele realized that while her father's betrayal still made her heart bleed, the welcome of her new family would help her heal in ways she hadn't dreamed possible four days ago.

If she were asked afterward what the holy man had said,

she would guiltily say she could recall very little. All she knew was that in less than an hour, her prayers had all been answered. A man...a good man had literally stumbled into her life. He'd taken her away from the dark place that had become her home, and now he was promising to love and cherish her for the rest of his life. And though Gisele had wondered if she might be afraid or nervous when the time came to tie her life to his, she uttered the vows without hesitation or fear. And as he cupped her jaw in one hand and pulled her close with the other, she knew her deliverance couldn't have been an accident. It was too perfect, she thought as he touched his lips to hers. No accident could result in this.

At the announcement of the nuptials, the city's citizens gathered outside the chapel and cheered loudly enough to be heard within the stone walls, and the afternoon was a blur as Julien and Gisele were given a feast, toasted by Julien's many allies and friends, and then were greeted by their many guests. More faeries than Gisele could count had attended, and nearly as many thanked her for catching the eye of the rascally young prince.

One of the older faeries with purple hair and twinkling eyes bumped her friend with her elbow. "She'll keep him in line," she said in a very loud whisper, which only made the other faeries laugh.

"I'm not *that* bad," Julien protested, but even as he did, Gisele couldn't help marveling at how boldly familiar he was with the most powerful beings in the realm.

But none of them seemed offended by his familiarity. "Mind your new wife," another one said, shaking her wand at him. "Mother Dove has told us about this one. If she can't manage you, I'm going to have to let Alziera turn you into a horse the way she wanted to when you were small."

"I've changed my mind," the faerie named Alziera, who looked slightly younger than the others and had a faint orange glow to her blond hair, gave them a dry smile. "He'd cause far too much damage as a horse. Have you seen what hooves can do?"

They all laughed again, but as the faeries began to move on, Julien leaned toward Alziera, and the smile slipped from his face.

"Has my father told you of the situation with her..." He glanced back at Gisele. "Relatives?"

Alziera's smile disappeared, too. "He has. And my sisters and I believe we have an idea of just who this witch is. But we've searched, and as she's no longer near, you should have little to fear." She gave Gisele a soft smile, her exquisite face glowing slightly as she did. "We're not giving up, though. Mother Dove will be near while we go in search of the witch. If you need us, let her know, and she'll make sure we get the message."

"Are you going far?" Gisele heard herself ask. She hadn't meant to ask anything, but the idea of these protectors, new as they were, being gone again made her stomach flip.

"Unfortunately, yes. If this witch is who we believe she is, her...interference needs to be ended soon." Her eyes glowed briefly, and Gisele shivered. But nearly as soon as it happened, the magic was gone, and she was smiling slightly again. "To your happiness, Prince and Princess. May it water your kingdom as rain."

After the faeries left, Gisele leaned into Julien slightly. "How much longer will we be here?" she murmured. She glanced out the window at the waning evening light. Twilight would soon come.

"My mother wanted us to have a feast for supper as well, but I chose something far more fun," he said, his breath tickling her ear. "Come on."

TWILIGHT HAD FALLEN by the time they escaped the palace dining hall and made their way out to the lake. Birds of all sizes and breeds serenaded them from the trees as they went. The temperature was unusually cool for early summer, making the air just so that Gisele could scarcely feel it, and the sky was a muted mixture of orange, pink, purple, and blue. She filled her lungs deeply as they walked, relishing in her newfound freedom as she towed him eagerly along the small cobblestone path that wound around the water.

"There," he said as they emerged from the trees, and he pointed to the center of the lake.

"It's a house...on a boat!" Gisele cried.

He grinned. "Not on a boat. It's actually built there, held up on stilts." He searched her face. "Is...do you like it? Is it too small?"

Gisele laughed and clapped her hands as she stared at the little cottage. For that's what it was—a little cottage perched in the middle of the lake. Flowers of a dozen colors bloomed on the vines growing up and over the stones as though they'd been there a hundred years. Two little frosted glass windows greeted them from the front of the cottage as he helped her into the little rowboat that was docked and waiting for them.

"But...how?" She gaped.

He winked at her as he rowed them toward the cottage. "It pays to be on a first-name basis with faeries."

"You mean, you were so mischievous as a child that they all knew exactly where you were at all times."

"Precisely."

They were at the center of the lake in five minutes, but the reality of it all didn't hit Gisele until Julien was helping her out of the boat and pulling her up onto the little porch.

"I had wanted to take you on a glamorous journey some-where exotic, but with us not knowing where the witch is, the faeries thought it would be safer to keep you closer to home." He turned and looked at the blue door beside them. "Besides, finding any privacy in the palace is just about impossible. And I'm determined to have you all to myself as much as I can."

Despite her heart suddenly beating in her throat, Gisele laughed as he swept her up and carried her over the threshold.

The cottage was even more charming on the inside. A large hearth made of stones already had a fire roaring inside it, and a plush couch and two overstuffed chairs sat before it. Thick rugs covered most of the hardwood floors, and a little table with delicate chairs sat in the corner near the back windows, though the windows were all currently shuttered. To the right, there was a large bed covered in thick blankets and countless pillows, and to the left, a large wooden shelf filled with plush, rolled blankets and more books than Gisele had ever seen in one place.

Her heart beat so fast she felt slightly dizzy.

"I...um. I can only assume you're tired of your shoes and jewelry and all of that," Julien said, suddenly looking nearly as shy as Gisele felt. "Would you...would you like me to help you take your jewelry off?"

Unable to speak, Gisele nodded and turned so he could help her remove the necklace. Then he placed his hands on the sides of her wreath and paused. "May I?"

Gisele smiled at the nerves in his voice, suddenly feeling much better about her own anxiety. "You may." Then she froze. "But I'll warn you. I'm not nearly as beautiful without it." She forced a small laugh. "My stepsister was always the beautiful one."

Julien turned her gently so she was facing him. "You forget," he said, scowling. "I've seen your sister. And she's hardly irresistible in the way you seem to think she is."

"That beauty was hardwon," Gisele admitted. "Apparently, it was purchased with her father's blood."

Julien shivered. "All the less appealing. No, I think I prefer..." He paused and gently removed the wreath. For once, the little birds were silent. Then Gisele realized they were gone. She held her breath as he stared at her.

"I mean," she said, trying to force a laugh, "you could use your wish to give your bride beauty..." She forced a laugh but felt like she wanted to throw up. She'd disappointed him. There was no other explanation for his silence. He'd finally seen that she—

"Why wish," he said softly as he bent his head toward hers, "for what I already have?" As the words left his mouth, he pressed his lips against hers. And Gisele knew she had finally come home.

FOURTEEN

Though Gisele never fully forgot her stepmother's threats, she was soon able to put them out of her mind from time to time as she focused on learning how to carry out the duties that came with the crown.

At first, she felt as though her own ignorance might swallow her whole, especially when she discovered that she would need to learn to read and write. But the queen was a patient teacher, and the tutors she brought in were unexpectedly kind and soon put Gisele at ease.

"You're learning quickly," the queen said one day when Gisele was able to read a line from a book. "It's only been two months, and you're improving every day. I—"

A knock sounded at the door, then a moment later, the door opened. Gisele and the queen looked up to find Julien beaming down at them.

"My two favorite ladies," he said, coming toward them. He bent and enveloped his mother in a tight hug, which made her squeal in protest as she tried to push away.

"Julien, you're *soaking wet!*"

Julien let go and stepped back. "Thank you. That just proves that my time spent with the swordmaster was well worth it.

"Julien!" his mother spat, holding her arms out and shaking them. Julien laughed and turned to Gisele, spreading his arms out wide.

"My lovely wife, how glad I am to–"

"I'll settle for a kiss, thank you," Gisele said firmly, holding her hand out.

"You're no fun."

"You smell."

Julien sniffed his shoulder. "I smell like man. A bold, powerful–"

"Thank you, Julien," his mother said dryly. "Now, was there a reason you decided to interrupt our work, or did you just come here to gloat in your own glory?"

"I'm hurt, Mother. Can't I–"

The queen narrowed her gaze. "No."

"Very well." Julien huffed. "I actually came here to tell you that Father has decided we're going on a hunting trip with the twin princes of Kadeem tonight."

The queen gave a start. "Tonight! But they just arrived! And I've had no time to have the kitchen prepare anything!"

"He said you'd say that." Julien grinned. "He says he's already sent word to the kitchens, and they'll have more than enough time to prepare what is necessary."

But the queen was already out of her seat and headed for the door. "Forgive me, Gisele. But my husband would think it acceptable if the kitchens sent our guests out with gruel. Excuse me while I see to this." Then she was out the door.

Julien turned to Gisele and took her hands, pulling her up from her seat. His teasing smile faded. "Are you going to be all right with this? My father is trying to make a land deal with the princes, and he's convinced that taking them hunting for several days will soften them up." His brow furrowed slightly. "I'll only be gone for three nights, but if you don't feel safe..." He let his words trail off as he studied her face, her hands still clasped in his.

Gisele's first urge was to say that she did *not* feel safe with him gone, nor did she want him to go anywhere near the deep woods with the witch still undiscovered. But, as the queen had firmly told her early in her training, the kingdom came before all. She had married into the royal family, and their duties couldn't be flaunted for personal interest. So she did her best to smile.

"I'll be just fine. I'll sleep in my chambers here in the palace and pretend you're up late for a meeting." She shrugged. "Besides, I highly doubt my stepmother would be so bold as to attack me here. And it's unlikely she'll know the trip has even taken place until it's already over."

Julien nodded but continued to frown.

Apparently, he wasn't convinced. So she tossed her hair carelessly and shrugged. "I'm so busy here as it is that I'll hardly have time to notice you're gone."

Julien's eyes gleamed. "Is that so?" he asked in a dangerous voice, wrapping his hands around her waist. Gisele's heart sped as he pulled her against him. "Well then, if you're so prepared, I guess I don't have to warn you that my mother plans on having a particular conversation with you later today."

"What kind of conversation?" Gisele tried to sound cavalier, but as she'd been conversing with the queen all day and nothing important had come up, her heart thumped slightly out of rhythm. What could be so important that the queen would set aside time to discuss it?

Julien's eyes glittered, and his eyebrows rose in challenge. "She wants to discuss baby names."

Gisele stared at him for a moment before laughing.

"What's so funny?"

"It's a good thing you're a prince and not a spy dealing with secrets of import. We had that conversation this morning."

This time, it was Julien who stared at her blankly. "You... you did?"

She smiled and nodded.

He continued to stare. "And...is that because...because we need one?" His voice cracked slightly.

Gisele smirked. "Not yet. But it's always good to be prepared."

Julien stared at her a moment longer, his eyes suddenly hungry, before bending and kissing her senseless.

"Your Highness."

Julien pulled back just enough to let out a whispered curse and muttered something about shutting the blasted door next time. Then he drew a deep breath and turned to face Samuel, who looked as proper as ever and not at all ashamed of interrupting such an intimate moment. Her face burning, Gisele looked down to hide her smile.

"Yes, Samuel?" Julien asked coldly.

"Your father has requested that you meet him at the stables immediately, Sire."

Julien closed his eyes. "Thank you. I will be there shortly."

Samuel bowed and headed out into the hall.

With a sigh, Julien turned back to Gisele. "I suppose I need to change." Then he pointed a finger at her. "But we are *not* done with this conversation."

"About what?" Gisele grinned. "Babies?"

"Yes. That one. I fully expect to pick up right where we left off the moment I get back," he said as he left the room.

"Then come back soon," Gisele called after him.

"Gisele!" Julien groaned from down the hall. "You're killing me!"

Gisele chortled to herself, wondering as she often did how she'd gone from a cowering captive in her old home to teasing her husband–the crown prince–in the span of two short months.

When he was truly gone an hour later, however, she wasn't feeling nearly as carefree. As much as she hated to admit it, his absence weighed heavily on her like a cold, wet blanket. For while he was usually busy, and they would often go nearly an entire day without crossing paths, since the wedding Gisele had always known he was *there*.

Her fear now was irrational, she knew. She was in the heart of the kingdom's stronghold, surrounded by guards and soldiers. And even if Julien was with her when her step-mother decided to strike back, there was likely very little he would be able to do about it. Still...

He was gone.

To Gisele's relief, she didn't have long to wallow in her anxiety. Soon, her mother-in-law returned, and they took up the duties they'd put on hold at the king's impromptu hunt. The hours began to pass quickly once again, and Gisele was somewhat able to pretend normalcy.

After supper that evening, she decided to get some fresh air and went for a walk through an herb garden that had been planted on one of the castle's larger balconies. Several other nobles were strolling the balcony as well, talking in hushed voices, so she found a bench as far from them as she could and leaned against the snow-white banister. Tonight's sunset was duller than the one that had been painted across the sky the night of their wedding, but it brought Gisele some comfort knowing that somewhere in the treetops visible from that balcony, her husband was looking at the sunset, too.

"Princess Gisele, there you are."

Gisele turned to find the castle seamstress walking toward her.

"Mistress Krystal," Gisele said, forcing a smile. "How are you?"

Mistress Krystal dropped a quick curtsy. "Oh, I'm well, thank you. I must apologize, however, for needing to ask you for your assistance so late in the day. I'm afraid one of the servants stitched your new gown the wrong way, and I'll need to measure you again."

Gisele blinked. "I wasn't aware I was receiving any new gowns." As she spoke, she felt a strange stillness settle in the air. She glanced at the other courtiers on the balcony, wondering if they had felt it, too. Then her blood ran cold.

Everyone was frozen in place. Every single one. Like living statues, they dotted the garden, silent and unmoving. At the same time, Gisele's little birds began chirping frantically.

She looked back at Mistress Krystal to find not the seamstress looking at her but her stepmother staring back.

"Adrienne," she whispered.

"Hello, Gisele." Adrienne gave her a cold smile. "So nice to see you."

FIFTEEN

Gisele's chest seized as she stared at her stepmother. The people around her continued to stand and sit, motionless as if they'd been statues from the start.

"Surely you're not surprised," Adrienne said, glancing at the people as well. "Do you think I'd sacrifice my husband for my daughter just to lose the largest prize to someone like you?"

"I...I never wanted to compete," Gisele said, thinking frantically. She nearly screamed for the nearest guard when she spotted him behind a bush nearby–just as frozen as everyone else appeared to be.

"Don't bother calling for help," Adrienne said, sounding somewhat bored. "They're all frozen. Every single one."

"Have you...did you hurt them?" Gisele gasped out. How much magic had the witch poured into that particular charm to reach every soul in the castle?

"They'll all be perfectly fine as long as you cooperate,"

Adrienne said, smoothing her dress. "Which brings me to the point of our meeting." Her green eyes hardened. "You really thought you could marry the *prince* and leave your sister to fend for herself?"

"I didn't know he was the prince," Gisele said. What was wrong with her? Adrienne didn't deserve this fear. And at one time, Gisele had been bold enough to stand up to her. But now...

Why did she feel as frozen in place as everyone under Adrienne's spell?

"I find that highly unlikely. Still, it's irrelevant." She took a step toward Gisele. "You *knew* how much I'd sacrificed for Simone! And yet you rode away as though you couldn't leave fast enough. How could you?"

"I...I did everything for you." Gisele struggled to find her voice, but she forced her shoulders to straighten and held her head high. "I owe you noth—"

"That's not how family *works*!" Adrienne screamed.

Gisele flinched. A mistake she regretted as soon as Adrienne's smile returned.

"Now, word has it that the prince is deeply in love with you." Adrienne snorted. "Something I rather doubt. Not that it matters."

"I don't understand!" Gisele said, annoyance finally warring with her fear. "Simone is beautiful enough to get any lord or duke she wanted! Why does she have to have my—" Gisele gave a start when her stepsister appeared behind her mother. She was glaring at Gisele, as usual, but in her hands, instead of her usual tea cup, she held a mask.

A mask that looked exactly like Gisele's face.

"The magic with which your rotten faerie bird cursed Simone–no need to look so surprised, Gisele. I know about your ridiculous bird friend. Anyhow, the magic with which she cursed Simone is a different kind of curse. One that, I'll admit, my godmother couldn't break. But," Adrienne's eyes lit up, "we have finally found a solution."

Gisele tried to think of a way–any way out. She could scream, of course, in hopes that someone had been left untouched by the spell. But that was unlikely, and it would make Adrienne think she had the upper hand. Well, more than she already did. Unfortunately, as they were on a balcony many stories up, there was no way out except to go back through the castle. And Adrienne was standing in the way.

"What do you want?" Gisele asked, hoping her voice didn't waver.

"To begin with, you're going to take us out to that lovely little cottage on the water. And if you even think of disobeying, consider your dear mother-in-law dead."

Gisele's blood turned to ice, and–as always, it seemed–her hands were essentially tied. That Adrienne would kill the queen, Gisele had no doubt. Which meant Gisele–once again–had no choice.

GISELE STIFFLY LED the two women through the palace and down to the lake, forced to listen to all the ways they admired the castle and the many items they agreed they would claim as their own later. Gisele did her best to lead them by way of the weapons room. Because of the ongoing threat Adrienne and the witch had posed, both the king and Julien had insisted Gisele gain some personal defense skills. She had no natural affinity for swordplay, but she had become quite good at hatchet throwing, though this had come as a surprise to no one. Unfortunately, her skills did her little good without a weapon, and as though sensing her plan, Adrienne warned her against trying anything foolish for the queen's sake.

Gisele had also hoped to see some sign of life as she walked, but it seemed Adrienne had spoken true. Every single person in the castle had been frozen in place. And by the time they reached the path to the lake, Gisele was despairing of finding any way out of whatever trap Adrienne was chasing her into. Then she had an idea.

"Go!" she hissed up at her little birds. "Find your mother! Go!"

"Gisele!" Adrienne shrieked. "What are you doing?"

"Dirty Creatures!" Simone spat from behind.

"Hush!" Adrienne snapped at her daughter. "That's what got you into this trouble to begin with!" Then she straightened her shoulders and spoke calmly once more. "Besides, it doesn't matter where they go at this point. We're here."

Sure enough, they'd arrived at the little dock where Julien kept their boat.

"Get in," Adrienne ordered. "Keep your back to me and face the cottage. I—Wait. Turn around."

Gisele, who had climbed into the boat, obeyed slowly so

as not to tip it. Adrienne studied her for a moment before nodding. Then she reached out and grabbed Gisele's rose pendant from where it rested below her neck. With a single yank, the chain broke, and Adrienne held the necklace up to study it.

"This has magic in it. Magic that could be very helpful for our purposes." She made Simone turn and tied the broken chain behind her neck. When Simone faced Gisele again, she was beaming, Gisele's rose necklace resting against her own chest.

Gisele felt her hope dry up as she stared at her necklace. She wore it so often that she forgot it was there. She wished she'd remembered it sooner. Whatever her stepmother had planned to do with her, if anything could have helped her, the necklace would have. But now, even that was gone. "What are you doing?" Gisele asked, her voice trembling with a mixture of fear and rage.

"You're right. You deserve to know. After all, this wouldn't have been possible without you." Adrienne smiled at her daughter. "Show her."

Simone lifted the mask of Gisele's face and tied it around the back of her head. Gisele drew in a sharp breath as the mask seemed to melt onto Simone's face, transforming her into a mirror image of Gisele. Triumphantly, Adrienne placed a replica of Gisele's wreath on Simone's head.

At the same time the mask slid into place on Simone's face, however, something else began to happen as well. Gisele was hit with a sensation of...What was that? Falling? No. More like...she was bleeding. Except, when she looked down, there was no blood. Not a cut anywhere on her body.

"What you're feeling is going to be uncomfortable, I'm afraid," Adrienne said. "You see, my godmother wasn't able to lift Simone's curse. But we found a workaround. You see, the longer she wears this mask, the more your essence will be poured into her. Including, I'm glad to say, your freedom from Simone's curse. And when the mask is fully attached, you won't be necessary anymore. My daughter will have everything I've sacrificed for and everything she deserves. She'll be free from that bird's blasted curse. She'll eventually settle into royal life with a handsome, powerful husband, and someday," Adrienne's eyes glinted, "my blood will sit upon the throne. And you," she patted Gisele on the cheek, "will have served your purpose like a good girl. Just like you always do."

Gisele stared at her in horror. Then she shook her head. "No. My husband will know she's not me. He'll–"

"How? Isn't this the famed faerie-blessed necklace the prince asked the faeries to create as a gift for his bride? The one he put a bit of his heart inside? It's going to pull him to the girl with the princess's face, just as it should. Just...not to you." She smiled at the necklace thoughtfully. "It's better this way, now that I think about it. Rather than a duke, my daughter will have a prince." Her smile grew. "And a kingdom."

Gisele lunged for the necklace. But in her haste, she forgot she was in the boat, and the boat tipped her forward faster than she'd expected. Still, somehow, she got one foot back on the dock just in time to hear the chirps of many birds.

"Dirty creatures!" Simone screamed, stumbling backward and ducking her head. But Adrienne wasn't frightened so easily. She grabbed Gisele by the hair and yanked her away from Simone and into the lake. Gisele felt a sharp pain as she hit her head on the dock on the way down. As she plunged into the lake's cold depths, the boat above her exploded into a cloud of splinters.

Despite the pounding in her head, Gisele knew she needed to stay above water...needed to find the sky to save her husband and her people... But she couldn't make her limbs move. Instead, she fell down, down, down into the darkness.

UNCONSCIOUSNESS SEEMED to have swallowed her ages before she could finally open her eyes. Her head only dully throbbed now, and she could move her fingers and toes again. But that was all.

Where had she been trying to go? Where was she?

"Don't move! I've only just gotten the wound closed!"

Gisele frowned. The voice was familiar. But where had she heard...?

She opened her eyes to see nothing but blueish-green light. Her hair, which had come out of its braid, floated gently around her. Water, she realized. She was being suspended somewhere in a deep body of water.

But why was she in the water?

Another sharp pain from her head brought back everything.

"She's coming to! Hold her arms so she can't thrash!" There was that voice again. Gisele tried to look around to see who the speaker was. Also...how was she breathing under the water?

"Gisele. Gisele, look at me, love."

Gisele looked around until she found a small, white bird perched on her arm.

"Mother Dove," she whispered, then gave a start as she realized that she, too, could speak through the water.

"Yes. My children found me just in time. But...oh, Gisele!" Mother Dove shook her pearly head and gave Gisele a mournful look. "The kind of curse the witch placed on that mask means you have very little time. And the more you fight or struggle, the less time you'll have!"

"I'm...confused." Gisele shook her head, but someone—or something—behind her gently forced her to stop. She glanced back, and though it was dark, she was rather sure she saw two large fins pressing down on her hands. Only then did she remember that Julien had once said Mother Bird could converse with all animals. Turning her attention back to the bird, she asked, "Why can't you break the curse?"

"I'm faerie-gifted myself, dear. Not a faerie." Mother Dove sighed. "I do know enough, however, to know that the curse has already begun. And if we can't get it stopped, you're going to be dead within a week."

Gisele froze. "What do you mean?"

"I mean that this curse works like a sickness. It feeds on you, taking on a life of its own. It sends your stolen life to your stepsister, stopping only when it's drained you completely."

Gisele tried to breathe, her head suddenly spinning again. She closed her eyes. "What...is there a way to stop it?"

Mother Dove sighed. "Death."

"The wearer's death?"

Mother Dove shook her head and looked down.

After a moment, Gisele said, "Oh."

Mother Dove looked up at her again. "I'm not giving up yet, though. I've already sent my children to the four corners of the world, seeking the faeries who went to seek the witch."

"You have to tell Julien," Gisele said. "He needs to know! Because if I don't make it, he'll have an imposter on the throne." Gisele could only imagine what her stepsister and stepmother would do when they gained control of a crown.

"I wish I could," Mother Dove said. "But, as I said, my magic is limited. If I leave you down here to find him, you'll die. The water allows me to protect you more than I could in the air. But only just."

"So, what do we do then?" Gisele whispered, wishing more than ever that Julien was with her. How had he only said goodbye that morning?

Mother Dove nestled down on Gisele's shoulder and sighed again. "We wait."

SIXTEEN

J ulien could hear the twins snickering behind him as the hunting party made its way back to camp.

"I don't think I've ever seen Julien ready to leave a hunt so fast," Edward, the youngest of their group–only by an hour, as he reminded everyone–remarked. "Two deer bagged, and he declares the hunt successful and finished."

Edwin, the older twin, grinned. "It's almost like he's got something better than us waiting at home."

"Better than us?" Edward gasped dramatically, running his hand through his short, red curls. "Unless...could it be possible that the famed heart-breaker Prince Julien has someone at home that he thinks is prettier than the present company?"

"Prettier than us?" Edwin made a show of touching his freckled face. "I'm rather sure that's not possible."

"I'm afraid there's no contest when it comes to that." Julien smirked over his shoulder. Most royals weren't nearly so familiar with one another, but Edwin and Edward were what Julien considered true friends. They'd gotten in enough trouble together as boys to keep that designation for the rest of their lives. "On her worst day, Gisele's smallest toe is far prettier than both of you mongrels put together."

"Did you hear that, Edwin?" Edward shook his head slowly. "He thinks his bride is prettier than us."

"I'll have you know," Edwin called up to Julien, "that I received no less than three marriage proposals during my walk through your city yesterday. And every single lady who proposed was nearly as lovely as myself."

"But were they as humble?" Julien grinned. His chuckle was cut short, however, by a strange twist...which turned into a sharp pain in his chest. Startled, he pressed his hand against his breast in an attempt to make it go away.

"Julien?" Edward called.

But the twisting grew tighter, and Julien wheezed slightly as he exhaled.

"Julien!" Edwin pulled his horse up beside his friend, all sign of mirth gone. "What's wrong?"

"My chest," Julien said, his hand still pressed over his heart. "I've never felt anything like..." Then it hit him. And as his blood turned to ice, he forgot the pain. "Gisele!"

He had turned his horse in the direction of the palace and was ready to send it galloping back when his father blocked his way.

"Julien, what's wrong?" he asked with a frown.

"He said something about the princess," Edward said with a frown, watching Julien as if he were a spooked horse. Juline felt like one.

"Gisele?" the king asked. "What about her?"

Everything in Julien was dying to bolt off in the direction of home. But he was a prince, and he knew from experience that things would fare better for him if he cooperated with his king. "Father," he said, restraining his heels from sending the horse speeding away. "May I speak with you in private?"

The king nodded, his brows furrowing deeper.

"We'll return to the camp then," King Leopold, the twins' father, said loudly. He motioned to his sons, who obeyed, though each cast a furtive glance back at Julien as they went.

"Son, what is it?" the king said once they were alone.

Julien pressed a hand against his aching heart once more. "Something's wrong with Gisele. We…I need to go home. Now."

His father blinked at him. "But how do you know?"

Here Julien hesitated. He hadn't told his parents of his wedding gift to his wife. But he couldn't afford to keep that secret to himself now.

"Before we were married," he said slowly, "I asked the faeries for a gift."

"Julien, that's an audacious request for anyone to make," his father said. "Even for a prince."

"Yes, I know. But I was worried about Gisele, and the faeries were more than willing."

"If you think this is going to comfort me," the king said gruffly, "you're incorrect thus far. If you knew the things the faeries have done to teach royals lessons…" He shook his head. "Pray tell, son, what did the faeries agree to give you?"

Julien hesitated a moment more, then said, "I asked them to give Gisele a piece of my heart."

The king blanched. "You did *what?*"

"It's in the necklace she always wears, the rose one." He took a deep breath. "Without the witch caught, I was worried about her, and I wanted to always know–"

"Son!" The king thundered so loud he made Julien jump and his horse take a nervous step to the side. "Do you realize what you've done?"

"Yes!" Julien glared at his father. "I do."

"No, I don't think you do!" The king ran a hand through his beard, then his hair. "Julien, that is deep magic! You–the only heir to the throne and the future head of the kingdom–are now inextricably linked to the target of a *witch!*"

"Which means–" Julien began, but his father cut him off.

"Which means if the witch desired to, she could do far more than hurt Gisele. She could potentially control the entire kingdom through *you!*"

"Which means," Julien growled, "I had best get *home* and see what has happened."

The king froze. "What do you mean?"

"Something is wrong," Julien said, pressing his hand over his heart once more. "I can feel it."

The king's face turned white, then darkened. "Then go. I can't leave yet, but...know that we're not finished with this. We'll be discussing this the moment I get home." The king whistled and two guards came riding up. "Go with him." Then he gave Julien a sharp nod.

Julien didn't have to be told twice. He started to urge his

horse forward but then paused. Looking back, he said, "You and Mother always wished I would grow serious about life and stop seeing it as a game. Well, I can tell you now that I've never been more serious about anything." Then he turned his horse homeward and urged him to fly.

THE HUNTING PARTY had only set up camp at the edge of the palace grounds, but the ride back felt like it lasted a year. As he rode, Julien imagined every evil that might be causing the pain in his chest. Perhaps Gisele had fallen ill. Or an enemy spy had made his way into the court and was holding her hostage. She had been teasing him about baby names only that morning. Could she already be with child? Julien knew little about pregnancy or childbirth, but he did know that they were risky at all stages. Not long ago, one of his dukes had lost a wife before she was even near the time of birth.

Of course, the darkest of all possibilities urged him on even faster. Perhaps...the witch had returned.

The sun had set by the time Julien rode up to the stables. He half expected the palace to be in an uproar when he arrived, anything to hint that something had gone terribly wrong with the princess. But when the stable hands came out with Samuel, as they always did, nothing seemed to be amiss.

"You're home early, Sire!" Samuel exclaimed, glancing behind Julien at his two guards. "Your father–"

"Is my wife well?" Julien rudely interrupted.

Samuel blinked at him. "Um, well enough. Although, I believe she has a toothache. But if you don't mind me asking, Sire, how did you–"

"Here." Julien handed him his horse's reins and climbed down. "Is she in her chambers?"

"That I'm aware of, Sire," Samuel said, his brows puckered.

Julien took the steps two at a time. As he made his way up to his wife's rooms, the ache in his chest sharpened ever so slightly. Samuel's ignorance as to Gisele's welfare should have comforted him. Samuel knew everything there was to know about the royal family. It was the only way the palace continued to run as smoothly as it did. But, as it was, this only worried Julien more. If Samuel didn't know that something was wrong–for Julien was certain that *something* was wrong–then Gisele might be in even greater danger than he imagined.

His heart was beating so fast he felt light-headed as he barged into her chambers and then her bedroom, making several ladies-in-waiting cry out in surprise at his sudden appearance. But when he finally laid eyes on her, he stopped.

Lying in bed with a large cloth bandage wrapped around her head and jaw, Gisele really appeared only...to have a toothache. She didn't seem to be in distress, nor did she show any signs of some darker force at work. When she opened her eyes and saw him, they widened with surprise.

Julien smiled and went to sit on the edge of her bed. "Not feeling so well, I see."

Gisele just shrugged and touched her jaw.

Julien nodded. "I heard. What did the physician say?"

Gisele frowned at him as though confused.

"The court physician," Julien repeated. "Did he administer any sort of treatment?"

Gisele just shrugged again and rested against the pillows, closing her eyes once more.

Julien stood and frowned. She was obviously in pain if she couldn't speak. But something seemed...off. That, and the ache in his chest hadn't abated.

"I'm going to go see my mother," he said, bending to place a kiss on her forehead. His mother would know better what was going on. But even as his lips touched her skin, he froze momentarily. Her skin felt...wrong. That was the only way to describe it. Like skin, but also unlike skin. Frowning down at her, he gently took her face in his hands to study it more closely. Gisele, however, did not seem to like this. She jerked away from him and buried herself in a mountain of pillows once more, facing the opposite side of the bed. Julien straightened and swallowed.

It was the first time she'd ever pushed him away. And she didn't even seem to care.

"I'll, um, go see my mother then," he said gruffly.

His mother, who was in her own chambers, didn't offer him much comfort.

"I tried to send for the court physician," she told him, "but she wouldn't let me. She locked the door and refused to let anyone in until I promised her he'd gone away."

"I tried to touch her, and she pulled away from me," Julien said. "She's never done that before."

The queen sighed. "Well, as much as I dislike saying it,"

she said slowly, "for I don't for a moment wish to insinuate anything about her birth rank, most peasants struggle to afford the help of a true physician. Most of the physicians in small villages such as hers aren't well trained, and many deal out useless remedies for coin. Mother Dove has told me many times about the false remedies the doctors present for the animals they're called to see. It's possible that a court physician might frighten her for being so different from what she's used to."

Julien shook his head. "But that doesn't make any sense. She's not shied away from any new thing we've presented her with. It's... it's out of character." The memory of her pulling away from him made his mouth taste bitter.

"You've only been married two months," the queen said with a soft smile. "You'll find many things about one another that surprise you." She smiled up at him and touched his face the way she'd often done when he was young. "Being married is a journey of learning to meet your spouse's needs before your own..." Her smile grew. "Even when your spouse surprises you. Give her time, Julien. She's adapting her life to yours, and she's come much farther in a shorter amount of time than I ever imagined possible."

Then she paused. "Tell me, how did you know that Gisele was unwell?"

Knowing the answer would lead him to another reaction similar to his father's, Julien only gave her a tired smile. "That's a long story for another day. I'm going to go see Gisele again now."

Though his mother had given him a long look, she only

nodded as Julien kissed her cheek. Then he returned to his wife's chambers.

The ladies-in-waiting were gone this time. Only a single young woman sat near the closed door, dozing lightly in her seat. Julien was careful not to disturb her as he peeked through the door at his sleeping wife's form. Even Gisele's little birds were quiet.

Once he was convinced she was really asleep, he made his way over to one of the large windows in her dressing room, one that faced the lake where they'd spent so many happy hours. Twilight was dying, and the east sky was a myriad of blues. The lake reflected those blues as it rippled in the slight breeze that rustled the trees. It all looked so peaceful. But Julien felt no peace as he continued to rub at the ache that had settled into his heart.

What did it mean?

A movement below caught Julien's wandering eyes, and he squinted to see better in the quickly falling dark. Then his heart stopped as a hazy figure rose out of the water.

The figure was as familiar to him as his own. It was the very figure of the girl in the room behind him, complete with its own hazy wreath. But unlike Gisele, who was very real, this figure blurred slightly when it moved. Still, it had enough substance to look around as though searching. Before its gaze rested upon him.

Not that he could really know what she saw. But her—its—face stopped moving as soon as it was pointed up at him. And the pain in his chest sharpened as he felt rather than saw them lock gazes.

How long they stared at one another, he didn't know.

But the second the figure took one step back into the lake, he bolted for the door. Tearing through the halls so fast he made servants cry out and guards call after him, he ran faster than he ever had before.

His chest felt as though it might burst when he finally reached the dock beside which the figure had stood only moments before. But he was too late. All signs of the silhouetted figure were gone.

SEVENTEEN

Julien stopped in his rooms to change out of his soaking clothes on the way back. Though the hazy figure of the girl had disappeared, the pain in his heart had ached more and more until he'd dived into the water to find her. But searching the water was impossible in the dark, and he wasn't even sure what he was looking for.

So, empty-handed and at a loss for answers, he put on dry clothes. Then he slept on the couch in Gisele's dressing room that night. Or rather, he reclined there. Try as he might, sleep couldn't come. His chest ached too much for that, growing worse instead of better. For lack of anything better to do, he turned the events of the day over in his head continuously.

Gisele's goodbye that afternoon had been perfectly within character. Every touch, every tease had been that of the girl he'd fallen in love with. But the strange tug on his heart was too strong to ignore, and the odd sensation of her skin against his lips from when he'd kissed her that evening haunted him. He knew the feel of her skin as well as his own. And the way she'd hidden from him as well as she could within the confines of her bed...

Julien shook his head. The sun would soon rise, and his lack of sleep wrought a determination within him that he had never felt directed at his wife before. She was *going* to see the physician whether she liked it or not. She owed him that.

Decision made, Julien stood and went to the girl who was still sitting on the chair outside Gisele's door.

"Please fetch the princess some tea and the palace physician," he told her. "I'll stay with her until you get back."

The girl curtseyed quickly and hurried to do as he said. When she was gone, Julien opened the bedchamber's door and peeked inside. To his surprise, Gisele was already eating breakfast.

She didn't see him at first. Her focus was fully given to her food. He watched with a slightly horrified fascination as she wolfed down the soft bread roll and then the cooked cinnamon apple pieces. She hadn't known all the proper uses for the many utensils the palace used at formal meals when she'd arrived, but she'd learned quickly, and now even his mother insisted that Gisele ate like a royal-born princess. But that wasn't how she was eating now.

Instead, she was cramming each piece of food into her mouth, biting down only when she couldn't fit any more inside. And her jaw seemed to be working just fine.

"It would seem you're feeling better," Julien said with a forced smile as he walked in.

Gisele looked up at him, panic obvious in her eyes as she realized she wasn't alone. Quickly, she ducked her head as she finished chewing and wiped her mouth on the back of her hand, completely ignoring the napkin on the side of her tray.

"May I see?" Julien asked, stretching his hand out toward her face. Instead of leaning into his hand as she often did, however, and smiling up at him with those morning sky blue eyes, Gisele scrambled back and shook her head, pointing at her bandage once more.

"But I just saw you eating," Julien said. "Your jaw was moving as if nothing was wrong."

Before she could respond, her attention snapped up to the door as an elderly physician walked in, his spectacles perched on a rather large nose and his usual smile lighting his lined face. Physician Alfred had been serving the king and queen since Julien's parents had married, and Julien trusted him more than nearly any other soul in the palace. Behind him came his apprentice, a heavyset, good-natured young man named Dolf.

"I hear the princess is ready to see me," Alfred said. "I will admit that I was rather anxious when I heard you wouldn't call for me last night."

"She seems to have improved since then," Julien said. "She was eating quite well this morning." A little too well.

"Ah, well, I'm glad to hear that. Dolf, my bag, please." Alfred sat on the edge of the princess's bed, but as he reached for his bag, Gisele let out a strange squeal and scrambled backward, stopping only when she hit the headboard. Her eyes were bulging, and guttural sounds came from her throat.

"Oh! Well, if you're frightened, Your Highness, I promise you it won't hurt," Alfred said in a gentle voice, looking far less disquieted than Julien felt. He held up another set of spectacles and placed them on the tip of his nose. "I only want to see you better."

"Dirty creatures!" Gisele shrieked, pressing herself back against the headboard.

The physician and his apprentice stared at her, their mouths falling open, but Julien felt suddenly as though he might be sick.

Dirty creatures.

It was exactly what her cursed sister had screamed at him when he'd gone looking for Gisele.

"Gisele!" he cried, unable to hold back his shock this time. "What...what in the–"

"Dirty creatures!" Gisele screamed again, her voice breaking as she began to sob. "Dirty creatures!" She hid her face in her hands and continued to sob as the physician and his assistant turned to stare at Julien.

IN THE END, there was nothing to be done for it. Gisele would let neither Alfred nor Julien touch her, and in the end, Julien had to escort the physician and his apprentice out, apologizing like he never had before.

"What was that?" he demanded as soon as he had shut the door behind him.

Gisele glared at him resentfully as she picked at a loose thread on her blanket.

"So you can cram food into your mouth and scream at people, but you can't answer a simple question?" Julien put his hands on his hips. "I need some answers, Gisele."

Gisele just sniffed and looked down.

Usually, Gisele's tears had the power to bring Julien to his knees. But this time, he felt...nothing. Nothing except the ache that continued to build in his chest with each passing hour.

"I don't know what is wrong," he finally said. "I know *something* happened after I left. I know that for a fact because I can feel it in here." He pointed at his heart.

Gisele's eyes widened slightly, but she stayed silent.

"And I *know* it has something to do with your stepmother or stepsister," he continued. "But I can't help you unless you let me *in*!" When she remained silent, he went on. "And if you can't tell me, I'm going to call Mother Dove. Or better yet, one of the faeries."

As fast as she'd run away from him, Gisele leaped toward him now. Grabbing his hands, she shook her head vehemently, her eyes wide and pleading.

"Give me one good reason why I shouldn't," Julien snapped.

If this was what his mother had meant about learning and growing together, he didn't like it. He didn't like who it was making him.

I'm sorry, Gisele mouthed. And, to her credit, she did look sorry, her blue eyes wide and shining with tears.

Julien sighed and took a step back to free his hands from hers. Just as her face had felt wrong to kiss, her hands...well, something wasn't right. "Can't you tell me what's going on? I want to help. You know I want to help."

Gisele bit her lip and glanced outside. Then her eyes widened, and she held up a finger.

One day, she mouthed.

"One day? You can tell me in one day?"

She nodded, and he let out a huff. "Very well." After a moment of staring at one another, he gingerly reached his hand out...and touched her face. And when he did, she didn't pull away. The skin on her cheek still felt off, but less so than it had yesterday. It was warmer and softer once again.

After watching her settle down for a nap, Julien sought out his mother to tell her what had conspired. When he was done, he wandered back to Gisele's chambers.

"Tell me if anything changes," he told the girl sitting outside her door. Then he went to the same couch on which he hadn't slept the night before and lay down. His tired mind wanted to chew over all that had conspired that morning, but his body wasn't having it. Soon he'd drifted into a light doze, and when he finally opened his eyes, night was falling again.

A tray of food—still steaming—had been placed beside him. Grateful, as his stomach felt hollow, Julien took a piece of cheese and bit off a piece as he turned to look down at the lake. And he nearly choked as the pain in his chest twisted hard.

There at the water's edge once again was the shadowy figure. Her silhouette was less fixed than it had been the night before, as if her body were more shadow than substance. Julien stood, transfixed as she seemed to search for him once more. But the moment their gazes locked again, his chest hurt so much he could barely stand. His knees threatened to give way, and he doubled over, groaning as his chest radiated pain through the rest of his body.

But he couldn't let her go. Whoever...whatever this creature was, he was sure it had something to do with Gisele's strange behavior. Gritting his teeth against the stabbing pain, he hauled himself down the balcony's railing and climbed down the trellis as he had the day of their wedding. He'd perfected climbing the palace walls as a boy, unbeknownst to his parents, and he was grateful for this skill now as he made his way down toward the figure that stood at the edge of the lake. But the moment his feet hit the gravel, and he turned to sprint toward the lake, the figure once again began to walk back into the lake.

"No!" Julien shouted as he raced toward her. But just as had happened the night before, she was gone by the time he arrived.

Feeling suddenly as though all the hope had gone out of him, Julien fell to his knees.

"Mother Dove!" he cried, his voice hoarse. "Mother Dove!"

But though he waited hours in the dark, Mother Dove never came.

EIGHTEEN

Gisele felt dangerously close to slipping away as she sank back down into the depths. She sensed in her bones that all it would take was the slightest push, and her body–or what was left of it–would easily dissolve into the water or float away on the air. She looked wearily at her feet. Last night, when she'd briefly transformed into her human form, her feet had been only slightly transparent, so that she'd had to squint to make out the rippling water behind them. But now...

Now they looked more like a screen than skin. And she could see right through them.

"I told you!" Mother Dove gasped as she dove down into the water to where Gisele had sunk. "Every time you resume your human shape, you lose more of what you were before!"

Gisele didn't answer as she felt her body shrink into something far more substantial again. A moment later, she was a small bird once more, no bigger than the ones who usually lived in her wreath but had been sent out to find faerie help.

"If you would keep your bird form," Mother Dove scolded, sounding every bit as tired as Gisele felt, "you wouldn't be fading so fast! And before you tell me you were only out for a few minutes, I could barely keep you in your human form for even that!"

"But then he wouldn't know it was me," Gisele whispered. Speaking had grown too difficult to use her entire voice. Mother Dove had given her a bird form in order to prevent her from fading away as fast as her human form wanted to do. But at this rate, not even that would last very long.

"The witch's magic is strong," Mother Dove sighed. "If you would only wait for a faerie–"

"They won't get here in time," Gisele whispered. "The curse will be permanent by then, and Simone will have everything she needs."

She'll have me, was on the tip of her tongue. But that thought was still too painful for her to utter aloud. So instead, she focused on breathing.

In. And out.

In. And out.

It was still strange to breathe underwater, and even stranger to do so in her bird form. But this was the best way Mother Dove knew how to keep her alive with the limited magic the faeries had granted her, so Gisele wasn't about to complain. At least, not to Mother Dove.

But in her heart, as she had done all day and since the

night before, Gisele tasted nothing but bitterness on her tongue.

She had never asked for this. She had never even asked to be a princess. All she'd ever wanted was a quiet life with the people she loved. And each time it seemed that she might finally be close, Adrienne happened. Her father had betrayed her. The people around her got hurt. And Gisele was humiliated once more.

Would this have turned out differently if she had stood up to Adrienne more from the start? Would that have done any good? What would her father think if he could see where his foolishness had gotten her? Would he be even remotely sorry?

Not that his treason would make much of a difference in the end. Once Adrienne had captured him within the shackles of wedlock, he would have been able to do very little even if he'd tried. The house and land and family might have been his in name, but Adrienne was the one with the power, and everyone had known it. So instead of standing up to her as he ought to have done–as any decent father would have done–he'd left Gisele to fight on her own.

And every time she and Adrienne clashed, Gisele had been sure that if she faced Adrienne ever again, Adrienne would surely kill her and everyone she loved. But after running and hiding again and again to avoid such a collision...

Well, a great deal of good that had done her. Now the man Gisele loved most in the world was in grievous danger, and Adrienne's spawn was very nearly ready to steal the throne.

Simone would have unspeakable power over countless lives. She would conceive and birth Julien's children. She would have every escape to the lakehouse. Every touch and soft word...

Gisele had realized early on that crying in her bird form wasn't nearly as satisfying as it always had been in her human body. And she hated that, too.

What happened to justice? she silently cried out in anger. *Was my life written to be a chain of tragedies?*

But the Almighty gave her no answer, and Gisele was too tired to continue shouting, even in her mind. So she slipped into the strange sort of dozing that overtook her much of the time she bobbed up and down beneath the water's surface. Just as she was ready to sleep, however, Mother Dove's tired voice broke the water's silence.

"Julien is a smart boy. He'll know something is wrong with the girl in your room. He knows something's wrong already, or he wouldn't have returned from hunting so early."

They'd only known this, of course, because several of the water animals had hurried to tell Mother Dove that the prince had returned and was at his window. Immediately, of course, Gisele had chosen to act.

Not that it had done either of them any good. He'd raced out and tried to find her, but her strength–and Mother Dove's–hadn't been strong enough to last, and she'd been forced to return to the water before he even entered the water.

"He tried looking for me last night," Gisele whispered again, almost as much to convince herself as much as

Mother Dove. "I have to keep trying. If anyone can save me, it's him."

"He looked," Mother Dove scolded. "But you were so exhausted you couldn't even swim to him."

"You could have tried telling him," Gisele reminded her.

"Not while I'm keeping you alive, I can't. You forget. Speaking to humans requires magic. And you're getting all that I've got."

Gisele, despite her anger, felt a twinge of guilt. "I'm sorry."

Mother Dove ruffled her feathers. "Don't be. Just rest. And keep holding on. When I found you, I knew I had finally found a woman Julien would listen to. And believe me, that wasn't easy. We'll find a way to save you yet."

Despite her kind words, there was no hope in them.

"The magic...will be complete...tomorrow night," Gisele breathed, nearly too tired for words. "I'll...have to try...once more."

If she didn't, it would be too late.

But, Gisele couldn't help wondering, was it too late already?

NINETEEN

Julien's mother put her sewing down and frowned up at him. "I still think you ought to find Mother Dove. She'd be able to make sense of all this oddity."

"I told you, I looked for her." Julien ran a hand through his hair. "She's nowhere to be found. In fact, there aren't any birds nearby. Have you noticed that? They're all gone. Every single one. Only those in the barns are still here."

"I haven't been outside enough to notice." The queen glanced at the window. The day was annoyingly sunny and bright.

A knock sounded at the door.

"Message for Her Highness!" one of the servants shouted. Julien went to the door and took the written, sealed note from the servant. After locking the door again, he returned to his mother's writing desk, where she was seated.

"It's Father's seal," he said, handing the folded parchment to her.

The queen quickly broke the wax and opened the letter. Her brows furrowed as she read it.

"What did he say?" Julien asked.

"He apologizes, but he can't return immediately. Something..." She blinked several times at the paper. "Something strange has been spotted several times just outside the royal grounds."

"What?"

"Here." She handed him the letter. "Read it for yourself."

Julien began to scan the letter. It was short, but the contents were so bizarre he had to read them three times.

"Apparitions?" He looked at his mother. "But Father doesn't believe in ghosts."

"According to faerie lore, there are many creatures that can take the appearance of apparitions," his mother said in a tight voice. "That he's seen any is concerning."

"And that he would see them *now*? Just when we've sent word begging him to return?" Julien shook his head. "You know this can't be a coincidence."

"And...And you're sure something's wrong with Gisele?" his mother asked. "You're sure that it isn't just pain making her difficult?"

"You've seen her!" Julien cried, gesturing toward the door. "The strange phrase she keeps repeating, 'dirty creatures,' is the same one her stepsister was cursed to repeat. I know it because I heard it myself. And when have you known Gisele to throw things at people? Or to make guttural sounds when she's angry? And the way she eats..." He shuddered. "No, this is the third day she's acted so, and with each day, she's less and less like herself."

"*That* I understand and agree with," the queen said. "But this woman in the lake you keep seeing? Julien, it's just so…"

Julien raised his eyebrows. "More far-fetched than apparitions?"

His mother pursed her lips. "I suppose you have a point. The question is then, what are we going to do about it?" She glanced at the place on his chest where he kept his medallion hidden. "You know, you could use your wish."

"I've thought about that, believe me. I'm afraid, though, it's like Father said the first time. I don't know enough about the situation to know what to wish for. I might wish for the real Gisele to appear in front of me, but she might be in some accursed sleep. Or in some other altered state. And we'd be no closer to finding the answer than before."

His mother studied him for a long moment. Then her eyes narrowed, and he gave an inward groan. "Julien," she said sharply, "what are you planning?"

Julien took a long moment before answering. He had to take care. He might be crown prince, but if his mother disliked his scheme, she still outranked him. She could have him locked in his room with guards on every side if she wished. And she might, judging by the look on her face.

"I've ordered the guard to clear and encircle the lake," he said slowly. "And I'm going to wait for the girl in the lake to appear tonight."

The queen stood and began to pace. "And if it isn't Gisele? What if it's the witch herself?" As she spoke, her voice rose in pitch. That was never a good sign. "And what if she bewitches *you*? Then uses you to kill your father and control the kingdom? What then?"

"I've considered all that, too" Julien answered. "And what I think is—"

"What you *think?*" The queen snapped. "Julien, you can't *think* something in this kind of situation. You have to *know*! When you're king, and you have the entire kingdom resting on your shoulders, fast gambles based on conjecture will get people *killed*!"

Julien blanched. He'd never seen this side of his mother. "Mother, you can't possibly—"

"I have been patient with you for longer than I can express." Her face had turned scarlet, and she drew herself up to her full height, which was nearly as impressive as his own. "But this is one conjecture too many! Your capricious—"

Something inside of Julien snapped.

"*Capricious?*" he thundered back. "Mother, have you forgotten that this is my *wife* we're speaking of?"

His mother opened her mouth, but he thundered on.

"You've said all my life that you wish I would take my position seriously. That I'd look before I leap. Well, you have your wish." He stomped over to the door. "I can safely swear to you now that I have never taken anything so seriously in my life. Because the woman in my wife's bed is *not* the woman I married. She is *not* the one that I chose to raise my heir with. And though I don't know who or what she is, I know that this entire kingdom will fall if I allow whatever foul spirit that is at work to succeed. And I will *die* before I watch everything I love crumble." Not waiting to hear his mother's response, he stormed out and headed for the weapons room.

His mother didn't call him back.

JULIEN'S LEGS ached from the crouch he'd held for hours in his hiding spot between two thick bushes several paces from the lake. The girl in the lake never appeared before sunset, but he didn't want to chance missing her. As the hours of hiding had drug on, the pain in his chest had begun to dull, but that only worried him more. This dark mischief—whatever its source—was strong. He'd felt that when the pain had peaked last night. And now, as it faded, he feared it was a sign that his beloved was fading too.

His mother must have at least been somewhat pacified by his passionate words because no orders came for his men to stand down. But as the sun began to fall in the sky, he wished desperately that his father had come home. He was a skilled tactician, one whom neighboring kings often asked for military advice, and his presence would have been a great comfort as the evening drew near.

But what Julien had told his mother was true. Never in his life had he felt the weight of his crown press heavier upon him. The girl he loved more than life had been lost, either in mind or body. The kingdom that looked to him for guidance and protection could easily crumble under the thumb of the evil he felt knocking at his door.

And though it might kill him, he would stand on the

threshold. He would readily give his life and breath if it meant extinguishing this darkness forever.

Or at least, as best as he was able.

The chain mail he wore was heavy and had made him sweat for much of the day. Several times, he'd even dozed in the bright sunlight. But as the dark and the temperature fell, the hair on the nape of his neck prickled, and he was more than thankful he had donned his battle gear. There was a chill in the air, far colder than it ought to be. And he sensed suddenly that something approached just as sunset cast a myriad of colors across the sky.

The world seemed to hold its breath with him as the light peaked and then began to fade.

Then twilight blossomed with its many brilliant blues.

And...nothing happened. No girl rose from the water. Not even a bubble appeared at its surface.

The moon was high by the time Julien began to wonder if he was too late. Was the magic gone? He knew he hadn't imagined the girl in a dream, as his mother had once suggested. If he'd only seen her the one time, he might be tempted to think so. But two times? Impossible.

The ache in his chest hadn't lied.

Then, as he began to wonder if there were another way to seek her out, if he ought to dive beneath the waves again, the water began to ripple. And he saw her.

The wreath crowned her head as it always did, and her dress was a simple milky white. Unlike the two nights before, however, the girl didn't slowly rise as though climbing a staircase. Instead, she stumbled forward, her knees buckling before she could stand.

Julien was at her side before she hit the ground. He grabbed her by the shoulders to keep her from falling. But the moment he touched her, his blood turned to ice. Holding her shoulders was like grasping the petals of a flower. As he gently lifted her upright, he found that she weighed nearly nothing. It was almost like touching a shadow. And when he looked closely, he found that her skin was translucent. He could look through her and see the gentle waves lapping at the edge of the lake.

"Gisele?" he asked, his voice choking on her name.

But she shook her head. "There isn't time," she spoke so low he nearly missed it. "Listen. The girl...in my room...my stepsister." She panted and closed her eyes, her feather-like body slumping in his hands. "Wearing...enchanted mask. Stealing...my life. Giving...to Simone."

Julien stared at her in horror. "How...what if I remove it from her? Will that work?"

She shook her head again. As she did, a small movement behind her caught Julien's eye. Mother Dove, who had also exited the water, fluttered unevenly onto a small rock beside them. She looked nearly as exhausted as Gisele.

"No time," Gisele whispered.

Julien looked at Mother Dove in horror. "What can I do?"

"The evil inside her is like a plague," Mother Dove said in a voice little stronger than Gisele's. "It's been infecting her, eating away at her and leaving its poisonous residue in her place."

It was worse than Julien's worst nightmare.

He'd spent months imagining all the ways Gisele's stepmother might get her revenge. But this was far darker than anything he could have ever conceived. He cradled her close, and she leaned her head against his chest. But she was so light by now that he couldn't even feel the pressure. And for some reason, that frightened him most of all.

"Once...finished," Gisele whispered again, closing her eyes as she rested against him, "She'll...have me. And I'll...be...no more."

Julien stared at her for a long minute. Then he yanked the wish from his shirt, struggling in anger as it caught on a button. But Gisele shook her head slightly.

"You can't save her with that," Mother Dove called softly.

"And why not?" He glared up at her.

"Because you can wish the poison away, but she will still be without most of herself. Or you could wish her to be whole again, but the poison would still be stuck inside."

"Then I'll wish this had never happened to her!"

But Mother Dove slowly shook her head, her own little bird knees giving out beneath her. "Wishes can't change the past, Julien."

"No one told me that when it was gifted me!" Julien stared down at his beloved's face, his heart falling into his stomach as he realized she was hardly more than a silhouette.

"Then I'll–" he began, but Gisele stopped him.

"Mother Dove...is right." She took a long, deep breath. "But...I think...there is...one way to stop...the curse from completion." She cast her gaze down at his side.

He followed her eyes then shook his head vehemently.

"No. No, I won't do it!" His voice trembled, and he knew his guards were all closing in and watching him. They had to be aware of his agitation by now. But he didn't care what they thought of him. What Gisele was suggesting was impossible.

He couldn't do it even if he tried.

"You must. For the kingdom." She gave him a tired smile. "For me. Let me…stop her. Let me win." Then her eyes grew wide, and her body convulsed. He clung to her airy form as she touched his face with a nearly invisible hand.

"I love you!" she cried out.

Then her beautiful form began to change. Her skin twisted and stretched as her sweet heart-shaped face contorted into the shape of a diamond. The pupils in her pale blue eyes began to elongate into slits, and two of her upper teeth sharpened and grew down over her bottom lip. She squeezed her eyes shut and moaned as her body's gentle curves lost their shape, flattening and condensing beneath her thin dress.

"Gisele!" Julien's voice sounded strangled. But before he could go on, a low melodic voice spoke from the path behind him.

"You'll want to let her go," a woman with bright red hair said as she approached. "She's fighting it, but the spell is nearly complete. And when Gisele is gone completely, there will be nothing preventing what is left from killing you on the spot."

"You!" Julien glowered at the woman. "You're her step-mother. Aren't you? Guards!" He looked around, but the places his men had been stationed at were now empty.

"Don't make this harder on her than it has to be," the woman continued, her eyes on Gisele as though she saw such a scene every day. Even as Gisele convulsed and cried out, there wasn't a bit of pity in the beautiful woman's hard face. "Let her go, and it will all be over soon enough." She paused. "It's not as though she'll *really* be gone. Everything she was and more will be waiting for you up in her bedchamber once again." She had the audacity to smile at him. "You'll have your beloved Gisele once more."

"That *harpy* is not Gisele, and you–" Julien stopped as Gisele's last words echoed again in her mind.

Let me win.

The medallion, which had pressed against Julien's chest for years, felt as though it might burn a hole through his armor. He suddenly understood what his wife had been asking. And for the first time since receiving it, he knew exactly what wish to make. Apart, neither her wish nor his would yield triumph. But together...

Together, they could win.

Gisele will be very angry at you for this, a small voice in his head whispered. He smiled to himself. She would be angry... but she would also be alive.

Gisele's body had continued to warp as he hesitated, but he bent down and kissed her forehead softly anyway.

"By law," he whispered, "you're the crown princess. Which means after I'm gone, you'll be the hope of the land."

"What are you doing?" Gisele's stepmother demanded, taking a step closer, but Julien ignored her.

"Take care of my parents for me," he continued, "and

our people. Marry someone who actually deserves you, and bring peace to our land."

Gisele let out another cry, one that was punctuated at the end with a hiss. But Julien didn't mind. He was going to fix this.

Removing a dagger from his side, he swallowed hard and closed his eyes, steeling himself before he buried it in her chest.

Gisele's stepmother scream mingled with that of Mother Dove. He heard the woman immediately begin to utter strange incantations and felt the air around them grow cold, but he kept his eyes on his beloved, blurry with tears as they were, and waited for his love to die.

"Julien," Mother Dove said as she landed wearily on his shoulder. "You stopped the curse!"

"I know." Julien watched as Gisele's body, which had begun to writhe when he stabbed her, without looking up.

"Then what did you mean about telling her to take care of the land?" She looked down at Gisele. "You know your wish can't bring new life for the dead."

Julien smiled sadly at her, the madwoman's incantations growing louder and faster behind him. "I know," he said. "You told me." As he spoke, Gisele's true form began to return. Her face grew heart-shaped and soft again, and her gentle curves filled her dress once more. What had looked like scales gave way to pale skin as her wild movements grew still.

"Then why are you smiling?" Mother Dove asked sharply. Seeming somewhat restored now that she was no longer keeping Gisele alive, she raised one wing in the stepmother's direction, and the witch's incantations turned into a gurgle.

"Because when we married, I asked the faeries to join my heart to hers."

Mother Dove gasped. "Julien! Do you know how dangerous that is?"

"I do. The faeries warned me over and over again. Without her, I will never be whole." Julien hugged his wife's still form against him, memorizing the way she felt one more time.

"Then if she dies—"

"I'm not going to wish for new life to enter her. I know that's impossible," Julien said. "But I can make another wish that can do what that wish couldn't."

As he spoke, Gisele drew in one more breath. Then she let it out. And she didn't draw it in again.

It was time.

He removed the medallion and held it tightly in the hand that wasn't holding Gisele.

"I wish," he said carefully, "for my life to be hers."

"Julien!" Mother Dove cried, but it was too late. The air around them began to glow, and Julien could feel the magic flowing hot and fast from the medallion up into the air, where the night's cold was replaced by the heat of summer. His legs gave out, and he nearly dropped Gisele as her eyes fluttered open.

"Hello, love," he said, smiling as he was forced to sit back on his haunches.

"What did you do?" Gisele looked up at the glowing air around them. "Julien, I died. What did you—"

"I made my wish," he said, his arms shaking so hard he fell forward and let her roll onto the ground. Then he eased himself down onto the rocks beside her.

"No!" She rolled over as he let his head rest on the ground. "No, you weren't supposed–"

"Weren't supposed to do what?" he breathed, lifting a trembling hand up to trace her face. "Give my life for yours? I'm rather sure that's what I swore to do from the start."

"But your people," she said, tears streaming down her cheeks, her blue eyes more vivid than he'd ever seen them.

"They'll have you," he whispered. "You're their princess now."

"I don't want to be princess. Not without you."

"I wouldn't have married you if I didn't have absolute faith that you could rise to the challenge." He tapped her nose before his arm lost all strength. "And Gisele?"

"What?" she sobbed, laying her head on his chest.

It felt so good there.

"If you ever have a boy," he rasped, his chuckle feeling strange in his chest, "Julien wouldn't...be...a bad name."

This only made her cry harder.

"And...Gisele? I wouldn't change a thing."

CHAPTER

TWENTY

The only thing that could have pried Gisele's head from her husband's chest was Adrienne.

Gisele's stepmother slowly pushed herself into a sitting position from where Mother Dover had knocked her to the ground, emitting a strange gurgling sound as she did. But when she finally faced Gisele, Gisele drew back in horror.

Where her beautiful stepmother had fallen, a new creature sat in her place. The only familiar part of her face that remained was her green eyes. And even they were altered. Everything else was like something from a nightmare. Her face was cracked by countless wrinkles. Not the wrinkles that came from wisdom and a life blessed with many years, but leathery and gray, unlike any natural aging Gisele had ever seen. Her limbs were oddly proportioned, too long for her body which was now misshapen and bent. Her teeth were a similar gray to that of her skin, and they were all slightly pointed. And though her eyes were still green—

albeit a mossy green rather than emerald—the whites around them were quickly turning yellow.

"What..." Gisele gasped.

Adrienne only laughed, the harsh gurgle sounding again. "I know you doubted my beauty. You told your father so more than once. Well, I'll give this to you, Gisele. You were never as stupid as he was." She slowly pushed herself to her feet. "You remember when I told you that I paid dearly for my daughter's future." She held out her arms. "Do you see what it cost me now? Not only the life of my poor, wretched, sweet husband, but nearly all of me. It was out of pity that my godmother crafted a new mask of beauty after I gave all that I had for my daughter." Her yellow eyes narrowed. "And *you* ruined it all."

Gisele got to her feet as well so she could place herself in front of her husband's still body.

Mother Dove raised her wing again, but her movements were shaky, and before she could release another wave of magic, Adrienne bent with surprising agility, lifted, and hurled a stone at the bird. Mother Dove let out a squawk and toppled off her rock onto the ground.

"Your qualms aren't with her!" Gisele said, her voice trembling more than she wanted it to. She sought to control it. "They're with me."

Adrienne looked back at her and tilted her head slightly to the side as she studied Gisele, looking very much like an owl regarding its prey.

"You're right," she said softly after a minute, another cracked smile spreading across her face. "My fight is with you. And it will always be." She looked down at her hands.

"I'm not going to kill you now, though. No, I'm going to make you suffer much more than that. Because you may be crown princess. But I'm going to personally track down every one of your family. Your friends. Your servants. Everyone you know and love...everyone you've ever so much as greeted will die a horrific, painful death. One at a time, I'll come for them. From the shadows I'll leap and then return, waiting to strike again."

She raised her hand toward Gisele, and Gisele felt herself being forced to the ground by some invisible weight. Her knees hit the rocks with a painful crack.

"You're...not the witch," Gisele forced out, despite the continuously pressing weight. She felt the strange desire to bow, but she fought it with all her might.

With all Julien's might, she realized. She, Gisele, would never have been able to resist such power. But her husband had given her his life, and with it, his strength.

And now that she thought about it, her husband had come prepared. Gisele bent her face to the ground, hoping her stepmother would just think her buckling under the weight of the dark magic that now filled the air. As she lowered her face, she quickly searched Julien's many weapons to see if there was one she might use.

"I wasn't...and yet I am." Adrienne chuckled again. "My godmother knew the faeries were closing in. So before they killed her, she passed her power on to me." She brought her right foot down hard upon the ground, and the ground around her rippled, nearly knocking Gisele over. "Which makes me perfectly able to exact the revenge I deserve."

Gisele moved her hands carefully about on the ground,

trying to make it look as though she was struggling to push herself up. Julien had strapped a war axe onto his leg, and Gisele's hand was so close. But freeing the weapon from his side would be the easy part. Once she had the weapon in her grasp, she would have to be faster than she ever had been in her life.

And she would have to be ready to kill.

This was no straw or wooden dummy, nor was this a trained warrior who could easily block her attacks with the intent of improving her skill. For while Adrienne was now as deadly as any human could be, Gisele was counting on the idea that she wasn't invincible. Nor had she been long steeped in her powers. Adrienne needed to die, and the burden of making that happen now rested on Gisele's shoulders. Doubt made her blood run cold, but she forced her shaking hands to try.

For Julien's sake, she would have to try. For the kingdom he had entrusted her with, she *must* try.

She glanced up at Adrienne to see her pulling a long, jagged knife from her long sleeve. Its blade was crimson, and Gisele could feel the evil emanating from it through the air. "As I said," Adrienne smiled as she began to stalk toward Gisele, "I'm not going to kill you. But I'm going to make sure you *never* forget who hunts you."

Gisele exhaled. *Now.*

She snatched up her fallen husband's axe. It was heavier than the hatchets she'd been practicing with in the training yard, but her muscles had been made strong by years of woodcutting. In a single movement, Gisele stood, lifting the axe with her at the same time her stepmother raised the red knife with a scream. A scream that broke into a gurgle as Julien's war axe pierced Adrienne through the heart.

Gisele watched Adrienne's body long after it grew still and her chest no longer rose or fell. She sat paralyzed by the many thoughts that ran circles in her head as her hands, the ones that had gripped the axe and sent it flying with deft precision, now shook violently.

She had faced off with her stepmother.

And she had won.

Adrienne was dead.

Julien was dead.

She, Gisele, would inherit the crown.

"I never wanted the crown," she whispered, though to whom she didn't know. "I just wanted the man who wore it."

"Such is the life we lead."

Gisele looked over to see Mother Dove fly up from the ground and then land upon the rock again. Gisele knew somewhere inside that she ought to ask if Mother Dove was all right. It seemed another lifetime that Adrienne had hit the bird with a stone. But from the way she now fluttered her wings, she seemed well enough. If she wasn't, she spoke as if she was.

"You are angry," Mother Dove said. There was no judgment in her voice. It was simply matter-of-fact.

"I was," Gisele admitted, staring down at Julien. "I was angry that the Almighty could have let this happen. That He didn't stop them."

"Oh, but He did." Mother Dove looked up at her. "He used you." She looked down at Julien as well. "He used both of you to save the kingdom from an unknown evil that was festering from within."

"I...know that. But it doesn't feel..." She shook her head. "I don't know what to feel." She placed her head on her husband's chainmail shirt, welcoming the way the metal rings pressed into her skin. This. This was something she could feel.

"Feel grateful," Mother Dove said gently. "Your time together was short." Her usually melodic voice cracked. "But it was more beautiful than what many people ever have in a lifetime." She paused. "And...know that this isn't the end."

"It feels like it is," Gisele whispered.

"I know. But in the many years I've watched suns and moons and kings rise and fall, I can tell you this." She fluffed her wings a little. "The darkness always comes in this world. And it always will. But after darkness...there is always light."

She didn't want to admit it. It killed her to admit it, and yet...Gisele knew deep down that Mother Dove was right. For even if Gisele was asked now whether she would have preferred not to love Julien at all...if she was given the choice to go back and do everything over again...

Gisele wouldn't change a thing.

Just as Julien had said, she had no regrets.

Of course, that didn't fill the gaping hole inside of her.

They stayed that way for a long time, Gisele huddled over Julien's still form with Mother Dove watching nearby. The evil chill that had filled the water in Adrienne's presence was gone now, replaced with the natural coolness of the night, and Gisele was contemplating whether or not she ought to try moving his body from the ground when the sound of fluttering wings filled the air.

She looked up to find the night suddenly as bright as day as she and Mother Dove were surrounded by a ring of faeries, their varying colors and lights making a rainbow in the night.

"So," Alziera, the one with the white and orange glow, knelt gracefully at Julien's other side. Unlike the last time Gisele had seen her, however, all smiles were gone from her face. "In the end, he became what all men ought to be."

"His name will go down in legend and lore," said a male faerie with green magic.

"That doesn't change anything," Gisele said, her voice suddenly dangerously close to breaking. "He's still *dead!*" The flood waters that had been held back by her shock tore loose, and she began to weep as she'd never wept before. "What took you so long?" she wailed between breaths. "If you'd been here only hours ago–"

"We wouldn't have been able to change a thing," Alziera said gently. "The magic was too deep. And he," she ran her hand lightly over his face, making it suddenly look peaceful, as though he were only sleeping, "made the wish himself. A very clever use of a wish, I might add. I'm not sure we would have been able to come up with such a scheme." She smiled slightly. "Although, from him, I would expect nothing less."

Gisele glared at her through bleary eyes. "You couldn't have broken the curse?"

"We're not gods, Gisele," one of the other faeries said gently. "We have strong magic, yes. But even we have limitations."

"I do wish we had been here. Truly," Alziera said. "We were across the world tracking the witch. We had just executed her justice when Mother Dove's children found us."

"She gave her power to Adrienne before she died." Gisele sniffed.

"Yes, we sensed it had gone out of her. But we didn't know where she had sent it." Alziera looked at Adrienne's fallen form, and her ethereal face hardened.

"Can...can you bring him back?" Gisele asked, fearing she knew the answer, but needing to ask anyway.

"I'm afraid we can't create life," the male faerie said. "We can...assist it. But we cannot create it from nothing."

Alziera touched Julien's medallion. "You can see what he did for you. He used his wish not to create life, but to give you his own. The bond he asked us to create before your wedding, where he gave you a piece of his own heart, was the bridge through which his life was carried."

"I still don't understand," Gisele said, tracing the shape of his face with her fingers. "I didn't have the rose necklace he gave me. My stepsister took it."

"Ah. Well, that's easy enough. The necklace wasn't the actual connection. It was only the tool with which the connection was completed. Once you accepted his gift for what it was, his heart was fastened to yours for the rest of his life. No one could steal it from you." She tilted her head slightly. "He loved you, Gisele. More than his own life."

"I wonder..." Mother Dove said slowly. Everyone turned to look at her. "Would it," she continued carefully, "be possible to create another such connection? Or rather, to use one already made?"

Alziera's eyes brightened. "What do you mean?"

Mother Dove glanced meaningfully at Gisele.

"Ah," Alziera said. "In that case, Gisele, I'm afraid I'm going to have to put you to sleep now."

Gisele sat upright. "What? Why?"

The male faerie gave her a wry smile. "Some magic isn't meant for the human eye. Some words not for human ears."

"You let Julien–"

"Julien was strong and well then," Alziera said. "He hadn't nearly died under the thumb of a dark curse and then faced off against a witch. And we still put him to sleep for the actual rite of magic to be performed." She lifted her wand, which also glowed orange, and waved it at Gisele.

"But..." Gisele began to protest. Before she could finish her sentence, however, her eyes began to droop, and she felt herself being lifted gently into the air.

TWENTY-ONE

Gisele felt the pain of loss in her chest before she opened her eyes. And when she did eventually open them, unable to put off facing the inevitable any longer, betrayal washed through her afresh as golden morning light streamed through the cottage windows. The sun had no right to be joyful this morning. She needed to mourn, and sky along with her.

Tears filled her eyes, and though she didn't wail as she had the night before, she allowed herself to cry, gripping the pillow that still smelled of him.

So lost was she in her grief that she nearly leaped off the bed when an arm wrapped itself around her waist and pulled her backward.

"What—" She twisted, ready to beat whoever had intruded upon her sacred place. And then she froze.

Staring up at her with smoldering green eyes was Julien.

Gisele opened her mouth, but no sound came out. And though her muscles had been wound like springs to fight the trespasser, they immediately turned to butter as he gently tugged her toward him again and cradled her in his arms.

"I don't...I don't understand," Gisele said, her voice cracking as she traced his face again and again, unable to comprehend what she saw and felt. "The faeries said they couldn't create new life to bring you back. They said–"

He smiled, though it was tinged with sadness. "They didn't."

"Then what..." Gisele had begun to shake, but suddenly, she knew, and with her knowledge, her trembling stilled. "Mother Dove."

He nodded and touched her hair. "As I did for you, she did for me."

Gisele stared at him. "The magic they wouldn't let me see." Then she shook her head. "But you had built a bridge between us when we were alive. Your heart–"

"Mother Dove had forged a bridge of another kind long before." He rested his chin on Gisele's shoulders and held her tightly against him. Gisele closed her eyes and let him, basking in the feeling she never thought she'd have again.

"How so?" she asked without opening her eyes.

"The faeries," he said slowly, "explained that while bridges between hearts can be magically and all at once, as I requested, they can also be created naturally. Parents, for example, nearly all build bridges between their hearts and their children. This often happens before the children are even born. And then there are the bridges built between close friends. And, of course," he tapped her nose, "the ones that are built between husband and wife."

"If they're built naturally," Gisele said slowly, "then why did you need to request that the faeries tie your heart to mine?"

"Because I'm impatient," Julien said, kissing her on the head. "I didn't want to wait."

"But...why is it dangerous then if it's so natural?"

Julien sighed. "It's always dangerous to give your heart away. Loving someone–truly loving someone–is naturally detrimental to the self. It means putting the needs of another before your own. But the bonds that are built naturally, slowly over time...the heart grows accustomed. There's less shock to the rest of the body and soul when it's called upon to pay its dues."

"But you're–"

"I told you," he growled playfully in her ear. "I'm not a patient man."

Gisele laughed, then settled more comfortably in his arms.

"Mother Dove," he said, his smile quickly fading, "unbeknownst to me, had built her own bridge to my heart. I...I didn't realize it, but she had chosen..." He paused and swallowed twice. Gisele gently squeezed the arm he had wrapped around her, her own throat suddenly feeling swollen. When he spoke again, his voice was deep and husky, and his eyes glistened.

"She said she'd lived many years, far more than any bird was meant to. She'd seen kings rise and fall." He gave a strangled laugh. "Apparently, none of them, however, had ever aggravated her so much as me."

Gisele squeezed her eyes shut.

"But," he continued gruffly, "she said that...she was never so proud of anyone either. And she wanted me to be her legacy."

They were quiet for a long time, holding each other tightly as the weight of what had happened settled upon the little cottage. But no matter how hard Gisele tried, she couldn't get certain words of Mother Dove's out of her head.

"I want to be sad," she said finally, "but something Mother Dove said makes me think that she not only knew what she was going to do...but was trying to prepare me as well."

"What did she say?" Julien asked softly.

"She said, 'Feel grateful.' And at first, I was frustrated because I thought she meant that I shouldn't mourn you. But now that I know what she was planning on asking the faeries, I can't help but wonder if she was sending both of us a message for when she knew she would be gone."

"That sounds about right," Julien said with a sigh. "Of course, it doesn't mean we won't be sad."

"No," Gisele said slowly. "But...I think it means we can be happy, too. We can rejoice in what she gave us...and the future she ensured with her sacrifice."

As she said this, Julien sat up. Gisele sat up as well and turned to face him. His eyes searched hers, though what he was looking for, she didn't know. He must have found it, though, because slowly, he gently drew her face to his.

"And for that future," he said, kissing her forehead gently. "For this, I will ever be grateful."

GISELE DIDN'T WANT to leave the cottage. She wanted to stay forever in her husband's arms, hiding from the world and everything in it. But there were shouts from the shore that Julien said meant the king had returned. They agreed that they would have to continue their conversation–and the many kisses Gisele still desired–that night.

When Gisele stood up, she realized that the faeries must have dressed her as well as put her to sleep. Instead of the dress that had been torn to shreds by the witch's magic, she wore a gown of white gauzy material made out of a cloth unlike any she'd ever seen. It glowed slightly, even when she stepped into the shadows, and unlike the many-layered gowns the queen insisted were the height of fashion, this gown was simple. And yet, it was more magnificent than any dress she'd worn before.

"Oh," she exclaimed softly when she looked at her bedside table. The place where she always laid her wreath was empty. But of course it was. Her wreath was gone because Mother Dove was gone.

"What is it?" Julien asked.

"Nothing," she said quietly, forcing a smile. "Let's go find your father."

He nodded and took her hand, and they headed outside. Then they rowed themselves across the lake in a new boat that was far nicer than the one her stepmother had destroyed.

Julien had been correct. The king had just arrived with his hunting party and was looking somewhat worse for wear as servants rushed to help the party unpack.

"Julien!" he shouted when he caught sight of them walking up the path. "Gisele!" He sprinted toward them. For a moment, Gisele wondered what he would do, and steeled herself for his wrath. But instead of shouting or getting angry, he grabbed them both in an embrace and held them close.

"You were right," he cried into Julien's shoulder. "And I'm so sorry I didn't see it!" Then he turned to Gisele and took her face gently in his hands, the way her father had done when she was small. And, just as her father had done, he kissed her forehead softly. "Daughter," he whispered as he pulled her into another embrace. And that was all. But it was all she needed.

THE FAERIES HADN'T BOTHERED to notify the king and queen of what had taken place within the castle grounds that night, so it was up to Gisele and Julien to tell them all that had happened. The queen wept as she heard what they had survived, and the king looked dangerously pale and crimson in turn.

Adrienne, it seemed, had sent strange apparitions to follow and distract the king after Julien had left. And though the king had wanted to return home, he had feared that they would follow him and endanger the palace should he lead them home. So he, his guests, and their guards had done everything in their power to destroy or chase away the silent bodies of light...only to have them disappear in the middle of the third night.

Around the time, they surmised, that Adrienne had died.

Throughout their storytelling, Gisele spoke only when necessary. Her words seemed to have left her, and she trembled far more than was necessary for an event that was over and done with. Never in her life had she felt more displaced. In some ways, it all felt like a terrible dream. And yet... holding her husband's hand, she knew that eventually, she would feel whole again. This, too, would pass. And for the first time since her father had remarried, she could move on without looking over her shoulder anymore.

Once their tale was told, a search was held for Simone. But she was nowhere to be found. For several hours, panic reigned as guards were sent through the surrounding cities and villages to find her. That evening, however, Simone was discovered tied and gagged in the palace dungeons already. It seemed as though, while the faeries hadn't deigned to speak to the king or queen, they had made sure none of the guilty parties got away. This annoyed the king excessively, but Gisele was simply relieved that all the missing threads had been found and knotted once and for all.

Or most of them, at least. Several weeks after, Gisele's father, Pierre, was discovered. He was found by a fisherman at the edge of a large river far north of their kingdom, farther north than he had ever been, Gisele was sure. To her surprise, when she asked whether she might see him, the king refused.

"Why not?" she asked.

Julien winced. "He's...He no longer appears as he did."

Then Gisele understood. Despite all of her warnings, her father had gone to her stepmother like a deer to a wolf. She'd sacrificed him for her evil wishes as she had her first husband. He never stood a chance.

Gisele didn't know how she felt about this. His betrayal still hurt. It would hurt for a long time, the queen told her gently. Probably as long as she lived. And yet, there was a relief in knowing the truth. Even better, she realized after, there was healing in knowing that once again, she had a father who loved her...even if he wasn't her own.

Instead of dwelling on the confusing pain within, Gisele did her best to focus on the good. With the witch and Adrienne dead, Gisele could breathe freely, knowing that the attempts on her life were finally over. So as soon as they could be spared, Julien escorted her back to her old village to convince her best friend to return with her to the palace as her lady-in-waiting. Gisele had wanted to do as much from the first, but fear had held her back. Adrienne had known of their close friendship, and Gisele hadn't wanted April to suffer as well. But now that she was truly free, she wasted no time in bringing not only April but her whole family to the capital city, where April's family soon opened a little store and found new wealth and comfort they had never dreamed of before. She also fetched Becca and Michelle at the same time. She had intended to fix them in a cozy little cottage near the palace, but April's family was so taken with them that they were immediately taken in to live with April's already large family. And when it was time for

Becca's baby to be born, a sweet little boy was welcomed into the many arms who were ready to hold him.

The greatest change that resulted from the ordeal, however, was in Julien himself. He seemed older than before. Slightly slower to smile, and a little slower to laugh. Often, she would turn to find him watching her with troubled eyes, and in the night, he often woke her with his nightmares.

She wished more than ever that Mother Dove was there. She would know what to say about Julien's new sadness. She considered asking Julien's mother, but somehow, Gisele got the feeling she wouldn't understand. They had tried to express to his parents what had happened, but there weren't words horrible enough to describe what had truly taken place that night, no expression dark enough to convey the depravity everyone present had felt in the wake of Adrienne's evil. So Gisele did her best to help him where she could and pray for him when she couldn't. She didn't expect the visit that came two months after the incident when she was alone on her bedchamber balcony, unable to sleep and waiting to watch the sun rise.

"You're mourning," a melodic voice said, making Gisele nearly jump out of her skin. She turned to see Alziera leaning against the balcony, twirling her wand in her hand and watching the orange sparkles it left in the air.

"Alziera!" Gisele hurried to drop a quick curtsey. "And, um... I'm sorry. What do you mean?"

"Your husband," Alziera said, tucking her wand in her sleeve and turning to face Gisele. "You're mourning who he's become."

Gisele blinked at her. "I'm...I'm not sure I..." She looked out at the city. The sun hadn't yet risen, but it was already bustling with people. "I miss him," she finally managed to say. "I mean, I'm grateful he's here, of course. But..."

"You miss the man you married." Alziera stepped forward to stand beside her.

Gisele just nodded.

Alziera sighed. "You're building your own bridge."

Gisele turned and looked at her. "Pardon me?"

"Your father-in-law was concerned when he heard that Julien had asked us to create a bridge to your heart. And he had a right to be worried. Deep connections—the kind that burrow down in your soul—make one vulnerable. And to have such a connection formed all at once through means of magic can be a violent shock to both the body and the heart. But what makes such connections risky, whether they're made quickly with magic or over time, is that they open our hearts up, making them susceptible to pain. You're mourning now because you've seen a part of the man you love lose a piece of who he was. He has, essentially, become a new man."

"I love him as he is, of course," Gisele hastened to say.

Alziera turned wide eyes on her. "Of course you do. You swore to do so when you married him. It can only be expected when you spend your whole life with another person that you will be witness to the inevitable changes wrought by time in them. And they in you."

Gisele considered this. She'd meant for her vows to last as long as life itself, of course. But she hadn't ever considered the vows to have so much...depth.

"But one day," the faerie continued, "you will look back and realize that he had to change this way. Just as you have and will be changed to become the person *you* were meant to be." She paused and smiled slightly, her eyes growing distant. "When Julien was small, the other faeries and I kept a close watch on him, as we do with most of the monarchs. Unlike many of the other royal children, however, he displayed early on the passion of a lion and the wiles of a serpent. We knew that he would be capable of great evil...or great good."

"Is that why you all know him so well?" Gisele asked. "Because you paid him such heed?"

Alziera laughed a little. "Yes. We–including Mother Dove–hoped that if we were a constant presence in his life, we could influence him for the better." She glanced at Gisele. "We also agreed early on that if one of us found a woman suitable for him, we would do everything in our power to throw them together. Loving a man like Julien wouldn't be easy, we knew, and it would take a special woman to manage the wild soul that raged within him."

Gisele looked back down at the city. "Did you know this would happen?" she asked quietly. "That he would need to die?"

"Not exactly," the faerie said slowly. "Most faeries can't see the future, per se. But after watching generations of man pass through this earth, we've learned that often–when an exceptional man or woman is born–a need arises that they alone were meant to meet. Before they can meet that need, however, exceptional as they naturally are, their dross must be burned away through trials of fire. Only then are they ready to do what they were created to do."

"So..." Gisele said. "He'll have even greater trials to come."

"But of course," Alziera said. "He's destined to be king. His entire purpose is to protect and lead his people at all costs. He is the wall that stands between them and the world's darkness." She tilted her head thoughtfully, her auburn curls flowing gently in the breeze. "You're not so different, you know."

Gisele frowned. "I'm not?"

"In many ways, your life has been hardly desirable. You lost your mother, and your father abandoned you to the evils of the woman who ensnared him. She waged war against you in every way possible, and when you finally escaped, she followed." She glanced at Gisele again. "You may not see it, but you've changed, too."

Gisele pondered this.

"Think back to two years ago," Alziera continued. "When your mother was alive, and your family was whole and happy, would you have been ready to challenge a witch the way you did when you stopped Adrienne? Would you have been ready not only to face her, but to put an axe through her heart, protecting not only you, but your kingdom too?"

Gisele thought for a long moment. "I...I suppose not." Now that she considered it, the faerie was right. Gisele had once feared her stepmother, and that was before Adrienne been granted the witch's power. And yet, Gisele had not only gathered the courage to face her once more that fateful night.

Gisele had stopped her once and for all.

"And now that you consider the past, if you could change it, would you?" Alziera continued.

Would she? That was an excellent question.

"I suppose," Gisele said slowly, "that while I wish desperately for my mother to be here…" She looked back at the palace and then the little cottage in the middle of the lake. "I wouldn't."

If her mother had lived, her father would never have married Adrienne.

If her father had never married Adrienne, Gisele's father wouldn't have asked her to fetch the abandoned axe in the rain.

If she hadn't gone after the abandoned axe, Gisele would never have met Mother Dove's little birds.

She never would have met Julien.

And if Gisele had never met Julien…

That thought hurt too much to even pursue it.

"See?" Alziera said, a small, triumphant smile on her face. "You and your husband have been brought through darkness. But in that darkness, you were forged into defenders of the light."

Gisele remained on the balcony thinking about what Alzeira said long after the faerie left. Familiar little tweets sounded beside her, and she looked down, smiling to see her little friends once more.

"I've missed you," she said, holding out a hand, which the

little birds hopped on at once. As they did, the sun peeked over the horizon, bathing the world in gold once more. Gisele closed her eyes and inhaled slowly, allowing the peaceful sounds of the morning to fill her senses. "I hope," she told the little birds as she opened her eyes once more, "that you'll always bring your little ones here. For I would very much like to know them."

The little birds chirped slightly before dropping into the tiniest little bows Gisele had ever seen. The sight made her laugh.

"There you are."

She turned to see Julien standing at the edge of her balcony.

The gold in his hair and unshaven jaw glistened in the sunlight. He wore simple brown trousers and a white shirt beneath a fitted doublet. And even in such simplicity, Gisele thought to herself with a smile, he was magnificent.

No, she wouldn't give this man up for all the world.

She went to him and wrapped her arms around his waist. He, in turn, wrapped his strong arms around her shoulders and pulled her tightly against him. Alziera was right, Gisele realized as they held one another. Julien had been changed by their harrowing adventure. As had she. But the man that had come forth victorious from that battle, while more solemn, was one she respected all the more. This man had scars. Scars that had been earned defending *her*. And never before had he seemed so much not like a prince—but a king.

Gisele's heart thumped unevenly in her chest.

"What are you thinking about out here all by yourself?" he murmured into her hair.

She just smiled. "Mother Dove was right again."

"What was she right about this time?"

Gisele smiled up at him. "After darkness…"

He didn't let her finish. Before she could utter another word, he bent his head and pressed his mouth against hers. First, it was gentle, but, to her delight, a familiar passion burned just beneath. His fingers moved from her shoulders down to her waist, then up her back to her jaw and neck, where he buried them in her hair. She could feel the heat of the fire that roared in his heart stronger than ever before as he pulled her closer still.

Finally, his breathing slightly uneven, he pulled away just enough to speak.

"After darkness," he whispered, his lips brushing hers, "always comes the light."

The Green-Eyed Prince

A Clean Fantasy Fairy Tale Retelling of The Frog Prince

KARTEK REACHED behind her neck and opened the clasp of the gold chain that hung there. Pulling it down, she carefully cupped it between her hands where she might see it better, and she examined the jewel in the sunlight.

The thick golden disk that encircled the pink stone had been carved with all sorts of ancient symbols, though few knew what they meant anymore. No bigger than her thumbnail, the whole pendant was the same color as the berries she'd tasted once in the northern realm, so bright in the direct light that it nearly hurt to look at.

Her mother had always made the jewel look so stately when she wore it. But after the sickness had taken them, when Kartek had been crowned jahira and the jewel had officially become hers, she'd felt awkward the moment Ahmos had put it around her neck, much like a little girl trying on her mother's clothes. And now she was playing pretend with the fate of the entire kingdom.

Kartek could heal, but she wasn't nearly as talented or powerful as her mother had been, and on that first day as jahira, she'd been sure everyone around her knew it, from the oldest alder to the youngest child in the palace. As time had gone on, however, she had learned to draw strength from the jewel. Wearing it was like having her mother near, and its subtle power imparted a constant strength.

"Couldn't you have stayed just a little longer?" she whispered.

Something behind her snapped.

Kartek jerked her head up and tried to turn to see what could have made the sound. As she did, one of the stones she was sitting on shifted, and she nearly fell backward into the well. She caught herself just before toppling headfirst inside, but as she did, the jewel slipped out of her hands. Pink and gold briefly sparkled in the sunlight before disappearing as it sank into the dark depths of the well.

Kartek stared down into the shadows in horror. Her jewel was gone.

"No! No. No. No. No. No!"

But it was too late. The gold chain and its perfect pink stone were gone. As if to seal her doom, she could just make out the shouts of men and the sounds of approaching caravans in the distance. Fadil and his men would be arriving back from battle soon. Most likely, there would be some clinging to life with only moments left to live. Others might have an hour or two. Hundreds, possibly, would need her healing if she was to heal the tribesmen as well. And without her jewel, they were all as good as dead.

"No, Maker!" she pleaded hoarsely, staring open-mouthed into the black bottomless well. "Anything! I'll do anything you ask! Just please let me have it back!" She briefly considered jumping in after it, but banished the thought before it was complete. She knew full well she wouldn't be able to get out again, even if she found the jewel. And by the time she got the proper servants out to search for the jewel, men would be dead because she had not been able to heal them. Besides, this was the desert. She was doubtful that any of her servants knew how to swim, let alone dive into a deep, deep well.

She wanted to cry, to scream. But try as she might, she could make nothing but a guttural choke.

Maybe if she dove in, she could find it and toss it up. She would die, but the jewel would be safe. The Maker would surely bestow it on another, perhaps one of her cousins, as she had no daughter of her own.

Without considering what she was doing, she leaned forward.

The people would be upset by her death, yes. Ahmos

would be enraged, hurt, and heartbroken. And yet, they might not despise her memory so much if they knew she'd died to bring hope back to her people.

She leaned farther out over the ledge.

"Did you mean it?" a soft voice asked.

Kartek nearly lost her balance again at the stranger's voice. Whirling around, she found herself staring into the most unusual face of a most unusual man.

He looked quite sickly with the skinniest arms and legs she'd ever seen, crouching beside a heap of boulders nearby. The hair on his head was mere stubble, and his skin was far whiter than even that of Kartek's allies in the north, so white it was nearly translucent. His only features that didn't make her wish to recoil in disgust were his eyes. They were a most unusual shade of green. How many people had she ever met with eyes so like jade? Nearly everyone in Hedjet and its surrounding tribes and kingdoms had brown.

"Do you mean it?" he repeated in a soft voice. "That you'll do anything to get it back?"

The sounds of shouting could be heard again from south of the palace, louder this time.

"Wh . . . where did you come from?" she asked.

"I can get the necklace for you," he said, straightening from his crouch and taking a hesitant step forward. "I'm a strong swimmer, and I know I could get your jewel."

"I . . . I need it," she whispered. With every second she wasted, more soldiers could be dying.

"I will get it for you," he said, taking another step toward her. "But I need you to keep your promise."

"What promise?"

"The one you just made to the Maker . . . that you'll do anything to get it back."

A wail went up from the direction of the healing tents.

"What do you want?" She tried to recall the last sum she'd heard from the treasury. It hadn't been Hedjet's best year in commerce, but surely she could—

"Three things. I need for you to vow to allow me to sleep in your bed and to dine with you every night. And," he kept his large eyes trained on her face, "I need the promise of your kiss."

"You mean . . ." Kartek licked her dry lips and gripped the edge of the stone wall to stay upright. "You want me to *marry* you?"

"Precisely."

"*Marry you?*" She was hallucinating. She had to be hallucinating. "I . . . I don't even know you! I don't know who you are or where you came from or . . . or even your name!" She gestured at his body. "You look like a northerner but you speak our language." Her voice began to rise to near hysterics. "Why would I marry you and entrust my people to a stranger? Or myself, for that matter?" The mere thought of touching his ghoulish body with its uneven patches of hair and spindly limbs made her shudder. The idea of getting close enough to produce an heir . . . No. She couldn't even imagine the horror.

The slight spark in his green eyes made her feel as though he could read her thoughts, but he continued in a steady voice. "Because if you do not, you will not get the jewel back, you and your people will suffer, and there will be no chance at healing or peace." He didn't blink, didn't even flinch as he spelled out her people's fate.

How did he know about the predicament of her people? And how dare he assume he knew best? She had never seen him before. She was sure of that. He couldn't possibly know what her people needed. Their customs, their aspirations, all the stories of love and hope that she'd heard while healing at the well, he couldn't know those. He couldn't fathom them. Heat gathered in her cheeks as she glowered at him. But then Kartek looked back down into the blackness of the well.

Still . . . without the jewel, she could not save her soldiers. She could help a few people, perhaps, but not hundreds. Not the thousands that would need it, should the enchantress attack a town or city. Kartek's warriors were strong, but they were spread out between smaller villages, the palace, and the capital city. And should the enchantress slaughter her warriors, her people would be defenseless. The entire war might be lost in less than a week. For who knew just what this enchantress could do? After all, she had decimated Gahiji and his men. Gahiji, who had been the fiercest warrior known to the Megal Desert.

And even if Kartek attempted to get the jewel on her own, she would most certainly drown before she ever laid a finger on it in the inky depths of the water.

Another wail went up from the tents to the north, and Kartek nearly shrieked for a guard. Surely Ebo wouldn't be so far off he wouldn't hear her. Someone would be sure to hear her. Then they would come jump into the well and fetch her jewel. But once again, Kartek remembered that not one of her people knew how to swim.

"Get it for me." She swallowed the bile in the back of her throat. "And I will marry you."

"And how will I know you will keep your word?"

She yanked a ring off her finger and shoved it at him. "This is my signet ring. It hasn't left my hand since the day my parents died because the alders placed a covenant on it to bind it to me. No force or coercion can remove it but mine."

He took the ring hesitantly. "So if I get your jewel and—"

"And I deny our agreement, then you can give this to my alders and they will know you speak the truth."

"And if I fail?"

She took a deep breath. "I suppose it will sink with you." She would never hear the end of Ahmos's lectures, but that would be the least of her worries should she lose the jewel.

He nodded and gazed down into the well. "Fair enough." Then he was gone. A splash echoed up to her from the well's depths, and Kartek closed her eyes and pleaded with the Maker to let him find it. And to also somehow save her from her awful promise.

She needed a miracle.

The sun remained at the same angle overhead, so she knew it was impossible for much time to have passed while he remained submerged. But it felt like hours. How long could he hold his breath? Could he really swim? *Let him live,* she prayed. *Let him find the jewel and live.*

Perhaps she was losing her mind, asking the Maker that he live so that she might be wed to an ugly little stranger who had extorted herself and her kingdom. But really, it couldn't be so bad to resent the idea of one more death on her hands. For by now she could hear that the caravans had returned, and the songs of mourning had already begun, echoing throughout the desert valley. She should have been there to greet them and immediately set to healing the sickest and the most injured. But instead she was here, agreeing to hand over her kingdom to a complete stranger because she had selfishly sought solitude when her people needed her the most.

Some Jahira she had turned out to be.

A splash sounded from below.

"Do you have it?" she called down.

"Not yet. But I think I know where it fell."

Kartek gripped the walls until her fingernails ached from scraping against the stones. The air rushed from her chest, leaving her empty and brittle. What had she just done? Her servants. Her people. Her soldiers. Her animals. The other kingdoms and tribes that depended on her oasis. Her future children.

Her own self.

She had just traded them all for a rock.

A gasp echoed up from the well. She leaned over its edge to peer down, just able to make out the shadow of a man emerging from the water. To her great angst, climbing the walls took him even longer than searching the water had. The stones were old and much of the mortar was soft and crumbling, so with each step he climbed, he had to stop and carve out yet another grip for his hands.

More important than anything, however, was the glimmer of her jewel hanging from his neck.

Kartek was shaking so hard her knees could barely support her by the time he reached the top. But instead of handing the jewel over immediately, the stranger rolled over the well's wall and collapsed on the ground, panting so hard she thought he might pass out, his skinny limbs sprawled in odd directions as he gasped for air.

"I promise . . . Princess," he gasped between breaths. "Our marriage can save your people."

Kartek frowned. Not only had he called her *princess*, which hadn't been her title in over a year, but the manner in which he addressed her was familiar, far less formal than even that which the alders used. Who did this man think he was?

But she didn't have time to ponder details. For as soon as he slipped the thin gold chain from his neck, she snatched it up and placed it around her own, inhaling deeply as the power surged from the jewel into her heart and all the way out to her fingertips once more.

She could heal them now.

"I suppose we will—" he began, but she didn't hear the rest of his words. She was running as fast as she could toward the tents.

Can young Queen Kartek and her surprise fiancé not only defeat the evil enchantress...but find a happy ending? Find out in The Green-Eyed Prince: A Retelling of The Frog Prince, a clean fairy tale novella set in the world of the Classical Kingdoms Collection.

Dear Reader,

Thank you so much for coming along with Gisele and Julien in their fight for freedom and a happily-ever-after. I hope you had fun! If you'd like more stories about them and other fairy tale characters, you can get them by becoming one of Brit's Bookish Mages by joining my newsletter team. You'll get free bonus content, sneak peaks, book coupons, and more!

And if you enjoyed this book, please consider giving it a rating or review on your favorite ebook retailer or Goodreads so other readers can find it, too. Thanks again!

About the Author

Brittany lives with her Prince Charming, their little fairy, and their little prince in a ~~sparkling~~ (decently clean) castle in whatever kingdom the Air Force has most recently placed them. When she's not writing, Brittany can be found chasing her kids around with a DSLR and belting it in the church choir.

Subscribe: BrittanyFichterFiction.com
Email: BrittanyFichterFiction@gmail.com
Facebook: Facebook.com/BFichterFiction
Instagram: @BrittanyFichterFiction